To Dorothy,

Joyful Christmas!

Becky Melby

Do You Know What I Know?
a Holly Park novella

Becky Melby

Copyright © 2016 by Becky Melby

ISBN-13: 978-1539536666

ISBN-10: 1539536661

Edited by: Cynthia Ruchti

Cover photo: Shutterstock

Cover Design: Becky Melby

Fonts: Times New Roman, Great Vibes, Playfair Display

All scripture quotations are taken from THE HOLY BIBLE,
NEW INTERNATIONAL VERSION® NIV®
Copyright © 1973, 1978, 1984 by International Bible Society®
Used by permission. All rights reserved worldwide.

This novel is a work of fiction. All characters are fictitious and
any similarity to people living or dead is entirely coincidental.

Connect with me online:
Website: *www.beckymelby.com*
To receive email updates on future releases or share thoughts or
questions about *Do You Know What I Know*, please use the
contact form on my website.

Facebook: *https://www.facebook.com/Becky-Melby-Author-
Page-147542291976020/*

To Bill
I love brainstorming life with you

Special thanks to:

God, for a reason to write.

Cathy Wienke, for forty years of friendship and taking the first step on this journey with me.

Cynthia Ruchti, patient friend and encouraging editor. Couldn't do this writing thing without you.

Cathe Swanson, for tons of advice, hours of formatting together, and a tour of the castle.

Jan Glas, for always being one of my first readers. Grateful for your friendship and food and the things you catch—typos, not colds or fish!

My launch team—I would name you all, but the group is growing and I'd feel terrible if I missed anyone. Love and appreciate every one of you.

Scott, Kristen, Reagan, Sawyer, Sage, Jeff, Holly, Keira, Caden, Zoey, Aaron, Adrianne, Ethan, Peter, Cole, Lilly, Mark, Brittany, Oliver, Finn, Weston, Leif and Laiken. You make life a joy!

❄

Chapter One

"*I* can't go to rehearsal. I can't look at him." Crumpled letter clutched to her chest, Bethany Schmidt paced from the bottlebrush Christmas tree in one corner of the church office to the door and back. Worn oak boards creaked beneath her striped-stockinged feet. Misty, her pink-haired friend, sat on the floor, painting her toenails and doing a fairly good job of stifling laughter.

Bethany waved the letter. "How can I be Mary to his Joseph with this on my mind? He'll see it in my eyes. My deceit, my betrayal. I feel like a prisoner." Forearm pressed to forehead, she sighed. "A prisoner of the heart."

"Wow." Misty Kowalski stopped stifling. "This is rare, even for you. Forgive me if I'm not as empathetic as you'd like. You know I love you, but as a pathetically single midwife living at a maternity home with a leaky roof and linoleum floors, it's hard for me to feel bad that you have to choose between the career of your dreams and a guy who's crazy about you." She picked at a smudge of purple. "If it's advice you want, knock down those prison bars, girlfriend! Ditch the job and go with the guy. How many men are going to look twice at a thirty-something single mom church secretary? This might be your last chance."

Bethany crumpled the letter and threw it at Misty. "But what if it's not a chance at all? We've only had two dates."

"Pastor Jay's been swooning over you since the day you moved back. And I have never used *swooning* in a sentence before, I promise. That's how sure I am he's nuts over you." Misty tightened the cap on the bottle of polish. "Why not just lay it all out? 'Hey, dude, I've got this great job offer in the Show Me State, so show me you love me or I'm outa here.' See? Easy peasy."

"Are you kidding?" She pictured the man with the thick dark hair that curled above his ears, the brown eyes that made her melt like butter on pancakes. "You know him. He'll say he wants me to chase my dreams, follow my calling. But what if *he's* my calling?"

"Since you're already doing the 'what if' thing, let's go with it. What if you take the job and say good-bye to—" The ringing phone ended the what ifs.

"Bethlehem Community Church. This is Bethany speaking. How may I help you?"

"It's me. Got a sec?"

"Of course." Her skin turned clammy at the tone of her sister's voice. She signaled her barefoot friend with a glance at the door. Misty was used to this. Confidentiality in the congregation and all that. But this wasn't church business. Misty padded out, socks and boots in hand, and closed the door behind her.

"I have news." Sarah's voice was hoarse, as if she'd been crying.

Please, God. She's been through enough. Endometriosis, three miscarriages, and a cancer scare. What now? "What kind of news?" Her voice squeaked.

"The best. We passed all our tests. We've got the green light to start the IVF in January."

Bethany plopped onto her desk chair. IVF. In vitro fertilization. Good news. The best. She put one hand over her face and rubbed her forehead.

"Bethy? You're not having—"

"No! Absolutely no second thoughts. Sarah, this is the best news ever! You and Dave are going to be parents!" As the news produced a latent smile, she stared at the framed picture on her desk. Ava, nine years ago, in a pink headband and onesie. Nine years and a lifetime ago.

"Well, we're going to try, right?" Shaky hope blanketed Sarah's words.

"Yes. We're going to give it everything we've got."

"You're the best sister in the world. Even if this doesn't work, I—"

"There will be none of that kind of talk." Bethany shook her finger as if Sarah could see it. "By this time next year, you and Dave are going to be hanging three Christmas stockings." She took a long breath and blew it out slowly and quietly.

As they said their good-byes, Bethany looked at the wadded letter in the corner of the office—a cover letter for a packet of I-9 and W-4 forms. A job in another city now seemed like a trivial obstacle to a budding relationship.

It paled considerably compared to the problem of telling Jay she might be only weeks away from being pregnant with her brother-in-law's child.

❄

"Hey Joseph, don't freak out about asking Mary to marry you because that baby's real daddy—"

"Cut!" Yolanda Holt, taker of liberties in script writing for Bethlehem Community Church, waved her red pen and fluffed her orange hair.

Misty, who did the off-stage narration, took a step back, feigning fear of red pen impalement.

9

Becky Melby

"Hey, Pastor Jay." Air jabs meted out each syllable. "Do you hear what I hear? Give the angel a little attention, okay?"

Jay Davidson blinked away thoughts of the brunette fidgeting stage left. Black skirt, red blouse, tennis shoes with yellow laces, eyes that drew him like an electromagnet and jumbled his brains, leaving him incapable of feeling the ground beneath his feet. Electrodynamic suspension. He'd read about it on a pop science blog.

"Jay?" Dante Estrada leaned down from the milk crate that somehow, at least for now, supported all three hundred-plus pounds of angel weight. "You need to take a break?"

Break. What she was going to do to his heart. Bethany Schmidt. Daughter of head elder Bernard Schmidt. Church secretary. Amazing mom. Breaker of hearts. "I'm good. Let's push on."

"Not quite the Christmas spirit, Jay." Bethany smiled a heart-cracking smile and glided to her mark on the stage. "This good?" She looked up at the man on the ladder with his hands on a silver canister and waited for his nod. As if she needed a spotlight. Couldn't they all see the glow that lit the room when she entered?

Yolanda's pen slashed the air. "From the top."

"Hey, Joseph, don't be—"

"I'm supposed to be sleeping, you know. The angel shows up in a dream." What was it about interrupting Yolanda he found so rewarding?

Hands weighted with gaudy rings and gold nail polish flew over her head as if they had a will of their own. "Nobody wants to watch you sleep, Jay. I saw it on the bus coming home from the rescue mission the other night and it ain't pretty. Why don't you lean back on that bench thingy and close your eyes then open them and look all trancy-like when Dante starts talking."

Jay complied, an act that gave his subconscious permission to project images of Bethany on the black screen on the inside of

 10

his eyelids. Specifically, images of Bethany saying no when he asked her out on their third date. Would the specter of doubt never leave? Was he destined to stutter every time he spoke to her? She'd said yes to the second date and gave every indication she'd enjoy—

"Pastor Jay? I got some coffee in my lunch box. It's from this morning, but it might help."

"I'm fine, Dante. Really. Where were we?"

"I was saying you're supposed to name him Jesus."

"Sorry. Again." This time he did it right. Right up until he was supposed to wake up, stand up, and take Mary home to be his wife. He made it to a stand just fine. It was the walking to her, taking her by the arm, and walking down the aisle part he messed up. Had there always been steps there?

"Jay!" Bethany dropped to her knees. Her hand caressed his forehead. "Are you okay? Don't move."

"I'm fine."

"No you aren't. I'm taking you to the clinic. What if you have a concussion?"

"I don't have a concussion." He grinned at her. "But just to be on the safe side, you should probably keep an eye on me for a few hours."

A *whoot*! sounded from the platform followed by a raucous laugh.

"Can you stand up?"

He nodded. The room nodded with him.

Bethany stood, held out her hand. "Come with me."

"Anywhere." Jay smiled. His head swam. Had he really said it out loud?

"Just to my place for some ice and observation."

The angel high-fived the lady with the red pen.

"No gossip, people. We'll leave the door open."

"But you'll be together." The floor shook as the angel jumped from his cloud, grabbed Yolanda, and began to waltz.

❄

"Give it to me straight. I can take it." Elizabeth Schmidt gripped the side of the exam table in one hand and a handful of paper gown in the other. "It's Whipple Disease, isn't it?" She leaned forward, daring Dr. Mae to tell her anything but the truth. "I watch Weird Diagnoses. I have all the symptoms. Hot flashes, nausea, bloating, fatigue. Or is it schistosomiasis? James and I went to Jamaica in February and I was so careful not to drink the—"

"Elizabeth."

"I'm sorry. I know, I always jump to the worst case scenario. Maybe it's just celiac. My mom has it. One time she ate a donut and all of a sudden she started hiccupping and then she, well you don't want to—"

"It's not celiac."

"Okay. Good. Can't imagine life without Cinnabon. So it's just stress? Managing a garden center the week before Christmas is like being in charge of the monkey cage at the—"

"You're pregnant."

"I'm what?"

"With child. In the family way. Bun in the oven." Dr. Mae winked. "Want some more medical terminology?"

"I'm forty-one! That's impossible."

"Clearly, it's not."

"But how? How did that happen?"

Dr. Mae perched on her stool. "Well"—her tongue made a tiny bump in her right cheek—"when an egg from your—"

"No! I mean. How . . . We thought we couldn't. Dr. M, *you* said we couldn't." A snort that was half cry, half laugh shook her shoulders. Her mouth gaped like a gasping fish, but she couldn't think how to close it. "Pregnant? A baby?"

"That's generally how it works."

"I'm going to be a mom?"

"That's also generally how it works."

"But I don't know how. And we don't have a nursery. The spare room is James's office and all of his trophies are on the shelves and jerseys on the walls and I haven't changed a diaper since my niece was born and she's almost twenty and what if—"

"What if you have the next seven months to figure it all out?" Dr. Mae pulled a pamphlet from a rack. "You're not due until June or July. We'll know more after the sonogram."

"Summer. Of course. It's not coming right away."

"I want to see you in two weeks. I'm sure everything is going to be fine, but at your age we're going to be a little extra vigilant. Make an appointment for an ultrasound sometime this week. That'll convince you it's real." Dr. Mae winked. "And call me if you have any problems or concerns. Okay?"

"Uh-huh." Dr. Mae left and Elizabeth watched her hands fold the paper gown, pick up her clothes, put them on, in a strange robotic way. As if one word had severed the connection between mind and body. Pregnant. She walked out to the reception area feeling like she'd taken a double dose of allergy medication. Fuzzy, dream-like.

I'm going to be a mother. Somebody's mom. Mommy.

Linda, a middle-aged woman Elizabeth had come to know years ago from frequent hopeful visits, stretched across the front desk and hugged her. "I'm so happy for you, Beth. I knew it would happen someday."

That makes one of us. "Thank you. I can't wrap my brain around this."

"Nice little Christmas miracle, huh? Let's get you scheduled for those appointments. I've got an 8:30 on Friday morning the 23rd for your ultrasound."

"That works." They set a January check-up appointment and Elizabeth put the dates in her phone. "Can I bring James for the ultrasound?"

"Absolutely. How are you going to tell him?"

"I have no idea. He doesn't even know I had an appointment. I didn't want him to worry if it was . . . Wait." The idea was delightfully wicked. In 1996, James had won a pass to the Green Bay Packer locker room. He'd asked one of the players to call Elizabeth for him. Four little words—the most important question of her life—and it had been asked by Reggie White.

Elizabeth suppressed a grin. "Would you mind calling him? Then I can record his reaction. Or give him CPR."

"Are you sure you don't want to tell him yourself?"

"I'm sure. It's kind of an inside joke thing."

"Then I'd be honored." Linda slid a paper onto the counter. "Just to make sure we're following HIPAA rules."

There were two sides to the Privacy Authorization Form, but Elizabeth didn't mind taking the extra time.

Linda would call at five o'clock and Elizabeth, camera ready, would be waiting—for sweet revenge and happy tears.

Mama. Ma. Mommy. She slid into the driver's seat and stared at the empty inches between the steering wheel and a belly she'd thought was just bloated. She placed both trembling hands against the space between her hipbones. "Hi there."

Elizabeth checked the pot roast and potatoes that had been cooking all day. She stuck a fork in the meat, then quickly pulled it out. She'd eat the potatoes. James could have the meat. At least it looked a little better cooked than it had when she'd taken it out of the fridge this morning.

At eight o'clock this morning she'd thought it might be her last non-Jell-O meal before a series of enemas and barium drinks preparing for endoscopic and colonoscopic tests and pokes and prods and biopsies. At eight o'clock this morning she'd started mentally prepping for Christmas in the hospital and losing her hair. Or her life.

Not gaining a life. Not once had that thought crossed her mind.

She chopped peppers for a salad. Red and green. She whipped up a chocolate mousse. Her stomach could handle cold and sweet.

Still half an hour until James would be home. What next? China. And her grandmother's silver. She opened the buffet and pulled out a table cloth. And the phone rang.

The breath rushed from her lungs. It was all a mistake. They'd switched her test with someone else's. Someone young and fertile. With a trembling hand she picked up the phone. "Hello?"

"Elizabeth Schmidt?"

"Yes."

"This is Columbia St. Mary's Emergency Room. Your mother asked us to call you."

❄

"I'm fine, Bethany, really." Though a guy could get used to this pampering.

Jay rested on Bethany's floral couch, feet propped, ice pack on his forehead, a mess of pillows behind his head. She'd been waiting on him for two hours. Waiting on him and picking her fingernails. Something was wrong.

"Let me check your pupils again."

She knelt beside him, and once again a wave of heavenly dizziness swept over him at the smell of her perfume. If he closed his eyes, he could imagine the couch had turned into a field of fragrant wildflowers on a hot summer day. But the heat wasn't coming from the sun. And he couldn't close his eyes because Bethany hovered inches away with a flashlight aimed at his right eye.

Becky Melby

"Is one pupil supposed to be the size of a dime and the other like a mustard seed?"

"Wha—"

"Gotcha. It's all good. Equal and reactive, like they say on TV." Her smile didn't quite reach her eyes. Was she worried about him?

"Am I discharged, nurse?" Not that he wanted to leave. A frozen dinner awaited him upstairs in his apartment. But he didn't want to take advantage of her kindness. Or rather, he shouldn't take advantage.

"The teens will be here in fifteen minutes. They'd love it if you stayed. We can talk after they leave."

"About anything specific? You seem a little edgy." Was she concerned about her daughter spending the week with the people who never had the chance to become Bethany's in-laws? "Worried about Ava?"

"No. She's having a blast. Her grandma's spoiling her rotten. But she'll be home on Thursday and I've got a lot to do. Parental Christmas stress, you know? So, yeah, stay. I need some adult company."

He was powerless. She'd said "need." What could a guy do but flop back in the field of flowers and enjoy the sunshine? "How can I help?"

"By doing absolutely nothing while I run over to the church to get some cups for hot chocolate. Do you have your phone?"

"Nope."

"Keep mine. Call the church if you need anything. And be my secretary if it rings."

"*How* long will you be gone?" He teased her with a raised eyebrow.

"A lot can happen in ten minutes, mister." She set her phone next to him and darted out the door.

Jay sat up. No dizziness. Maybe that was just because the source of his head spinning had walked out the door. He looked around, soaking up the feel of her. Decades earlier, the two-story apartment building they called the Enterprise had been the Sunday school wing of the church. His apartment, directly above hers, was a mirror image, but much less welcoming.

Jelly bean colors. Everything in the room, including the second hand couch, looked like it had spilled out of an Easter basket. Pillows the exact yellow of Peeps chicks, a purple blanket, pink pillows, blue walls. Nothing red or green on the white Christmas tree. Pastel lights and pink tinsel. Resurrection and new birth all jumbled together.

Out on the street a car horn blared and someone yelled words Jay wished he could edit with a string of bleeps. Seven years ago, when he'd come to Bethlehem as an associate pastor, most Friday nights started with a string of bleeps. Things were quieter now.

He opened the front cover of a magazine, but Bethany's phone rang before he read the first word. He answered it. "Bethany's phone."

"Hi. This is Dr. M's office. Calling to report that Beth's pregnancy test was positive."

"Her . . . *what*?"

"Pregnancy test."

Jay laughed. "I'm sorry, miss, I'm afraid you have the wrong number."

"Beth Schmidt?"

"Yes, but—" Sarah called her Beth. So did Misty. Had to be a prank. "Very funny. Who is this?"

"A bit of a shock?" The girl's high-pitched voice fired his synapses like squeaking Styrofoam.

Shock? If this weren't some crazy mix-up he'd be struck dumb or catatonic. "Wait. No." Had to be a mistake. The doctor's office wouldn't call Bethany's phone and give test results to just

Becky Melby

anyone who answered. "You'd better figure out who you're supposed to be calling, miss. You're breaking HIPAA laws."

"She signed a release. She's there, right?"

"No she's not."

"Oh no. I'm sorry. This is James, right?"

Jay slammed back against the couch. He'd been named for the man who disowned him. Bethany was one of the few who knew that. "Y-yes. It is."

"No mistake, sir. Beth Schmidt is pregnant."

Chapter Two

"I 'm back. Did Brian call?" Bethany set the stack of cups on the counter. "I forgot he was going to let me know if—"

"No. Not Brian."

The tone of his voice, flat and gravelly, made her turn. Jay didn't look good. Bethany dropped her keys and rushed over to him. "Jay? How are you feeling?"

He stared past her. A blank stare at first, then it changed into what she could only label shock. She scanned the room, panic building. Had she left something out? A letter from her maybe employer? A pamphlet on IVF or her medical records? A letter from Peter? Not that, for sure. She'd burned those "I made a mistake and I want you back" letters months ago. And besides, she'd told Jay about him before their first date. So what was it? "Someone else called?"

He gave a vague nod.

Had to be about the job. No one would give her medical information to him. Someone had called about the job. He'd found out she'd accepted it. But that wouldn't cause a look like this, would it? Maybe he'd be hurt. Or angry. Most likely angry. But Jay had the look of someone who'd just heard some horrible news. Or maybe the look of someone with a concussion. Had she missed the signs? She'd been a fool to let him talk her out of taking him to the ER.

"Jay? What happened? You're scaring me. Is it your head? Tell me how you feel. Are you sure you don't need to see a doctor?"

"No doctor. Not for me anyway." Sarcasm laced his voice. His eyes narrowed. "I'm going home."

Now who was the edgy one? He must have a concussion. "I think you should stay here. And I think we should call the—"

"Bethany"—his eyes locked on hers, disbelief in his eyes— "why would you—" A knock at the door stopped him.

MacKenzie Adams walked in, arms strung with grocery bags, followed by Brian and a guitar-toting friend.

"Hey, Pastor Jay." Brian strode over to him. "This is Derek. You bring your bongos, Pastor? Derek, you gotta hear him play these drums. He's . . ."

Bethany turned to help MacKenzie, who'd already started slicing buns. "What can I do?"

"If you want to finish this, I'll tweak the coleslaw. The dressing's too thick. It needs something."

The brainless tasks of slicing buns and arranging paper plates and napkins left too many neurons free to focus on Jay. And Sarah. And the letter. One thing at a time. What was wrong with Jay? Should she call a doctor? Something wasn't right.

"So. You and Pastor Jay, huh?" MacKenzie smirked over her shoulder from the open refrigerator door. "Heard you two were at the Cove."

"Maybe. I mean yes, we were there. Not sure if there's a me and Pastor Jay."

"Well, there should be a you and him. You two are perfect for each other. Can I do your hair for the wedding?"

Do You Know What I Know?

MacKenzie ducked and laughed as a paper plate sailed at her. "I'll take that as a yes."

The rest of the evening was filled with music and food and laughter. And questions. Jay didn't talk to her once. He stayed on the couch with a little huddle of musicians around him. Brian asked if he could empty the drawer under the coffee table and Jay played it like a drum, accompanying the Christmas carols that should have filled Bethany with joy. But something about Jay was stealing it.

He seemed normal with the kids, like he was having a good time. Until he looked at her. Every time their eyes met, he turned away. And each time she read something different in them.

Lord, what have I done? Was he really just upset that she'd insisted he stay when he wanted to go home and rest? Maybe he had a splitting headache and was too macho to admit to it.

Bethany Schmidt wasn't a game-player. She'd pin Jay down and ask him the moment the last kids left.

But when that time came, Jay left with them.

❊

Elizabeth held her mother's hand and counted IV drops, foot tapping with each drip.

Blood sugar. Figures her mother would choose this day to polish off a bag of gluten-free cookies for breakfast and then skip lunch. Mom was fine, but the nurse had asked Elizabeth to stay until all of the blood work came back. "In case we missed something."

Just give her some orange juice and send her home. She'd called her dad. He was on his way, stuck in traffic. She watched the second hand on the white-faced clock jerk to 4:40 and counted beige floor tiles.

James was home. She'd sent him a text about her mom. He'd answered, saying he'd wait to have dinner with her. In twenty minutes, the phone would ring. She'd miss it. No celebrating the moment together. No laughing over getting even. No recording to show their child when he or she grew up.

The curtain flew open. "Beth!" Her dad hugged her, but his eyes were on the gurney.

"She's fine—just waiting for all the tests—nothing to worry about—gotta run." She kissed her mom on the forehead—"Call you later!"—and whipped through the curtain before either of her parents had the presence of mind to ask her to stay. Worst daughter ever.

She rested her hand on her belly. "You'll treat your mama better than this, won't you?"

Southbound traffic rolled in slow motion while the clock on the dash seemed to speed up. By the time she pulled into the garage next to James's car, she had most of her mom's symptoms. Shaky, clammy, agitated. She'd expected a call from James. *Elizabeth, we're pregnant? After all this time?* But he hadn't called.

She opened the car window before closing the garage. The bracing air calmed her nerves. A little. He would be happy, wouldn't—?

Next to the step. A green bottle. Gold foil around the neck. Chilling in the cold.

How can a person laugh and cry at the same time? Elizabeth stepped out, swiping a happy tear. "I think we'll name you Joy." There must be a Latin or Greek or Hebrew version that would sound boy-ish. Or maybe they'd add an e and make it Joey. *But for now, little one, you are Joy.*

"I'm home!" She walked through the back hall, kicking off shoes as she went. "Traffic was—"

James leaned across the table, lighting candles in silver holders. "Welcome home, Mrs. Schmidt." He pulled out a chair. "Please be seated. We have some things to celebrate tonight."

The breath she'd been holding exhaled on a giggle. "We do, do we?" She tiptoed up for a kiss before taking the proffered chair.

"Yes, we do." He took their empty plates, returned with a 5-star-worthy presentation of the meal she had prepared. "First off, congratulations to you, my dear, for an accomplishment we thought might never happen." He winked as he sat across from her. "I couldn't have done it without you."

"I should say not." She giggled again. "What else are we celebrating?"

"Not only a promotion, but a raise *and* a bonus." He poured the wine. She probably shouldn't have any, but she didn't want to spoil the moment. "How's that for timing? With the money we've already set aside, we are good to go."

Good to go. Yes. *Did you hear that, Joy?*

❄

Jay's stomach growled, but the smell coming from the oven wasn't appealing. Still, he had to eat. He hadn't been able to stomach anything last night. An empty stomach, a night of little sleep, combined with the bump on his head and the crack in his heart to make him totally unfit for the adoption ceremony he was scheduled to perform in five hours.

He couldn't dislodge the words that had played and replayed in his head for hours.

How could I have been so wrong about her?

Bethany Schmidt. Daughter of Elder Bernard. Church secretary. Fantastic mom. Jesus-follower. Giver, mentor, role-model, molder of young minds . . .

Was *pregnant*?

Honesty. She'd claimed to want to start their relationship—friendship or otherwise—with total transparency. No skeletons.

Just a baby.

Jay opened the oven door. The scalding heat did nothing to warm the chill that seemed to seep into the marrow of his bones. He reached for the pot pie, realizing too late a person needed a hot pad to extract a metal pan from a 425 degree oven.

Seconds later, he stared at the splatters of chicken, peas, and gravy on the oven door as he ran cold water over his hand. He wasn't hungry anyway. How could he be?

What a sucker he'd been, wearing his heart on his sleeve. She was in trouble and he was an easy target.

Had she even told the Chicago guy he was going to be a father? What was his name? Paul? Peter? One of the apostles. Not Judas, but probably should be. Not a bad person, just not fond of commitment. He had come back while she was in the middle of packing to move back to Milwaukee. He'd made a mistake, he'd said. Had they both made a big one—a big, nine-months-and-a-lifetime-worth-of-commitment mistake—before she decided to dump him for good?

But Bethany had been living here since July. His Master of Divinity degree hadn't educated him about such things, but he'd had more contact with pregnant women since they'd opened Serenity, the maternity home across the street, than any man should have to. If Bethany were more than five months along, something about that perfect silhouette would have changed.

What if it wasn't the apostle guy? A single woman living in this part of the city . . . anything could have happened. She had to have been lonely when she first moved back. Had someone sweet-talked her or . . .?

Jay shuddered, pulled his hand from the running water, and yanked the towel from its hook as a collage of awful possibilities flashed before him.

Bethany. Why didn't you tell me?

Why had he been so quick to let anger be his go-to emotion? Why not compassion? What if Bethany was terrified? Or ashamed. Or desperate.

What if God was calling on him to play the role of Joseph in real life? To be the kind of man of honor who would stand beside her and protect her from the stares and the whispers, to be the one she could turn to when fears or shame overwhelmed her.

To be a father to a fatherless child.

And here he'd responded with cold rejection, with walking out of her apartment without even a good-bye.

He picked up the phone, set it down, breathed a prayer for strength, and reached for it again.

Bethany curled in the corner of the couch, blanket pulled to her chin. She'd spent the night here. Here and on the octagon tiles in the bathroom.

MacKenzie. It had to be her fault. What had she pulled from the fridge to "tweak" the coleslaw? A groan ruffled the blanket. There was milk in the fridge for the hot chocolate. Milk. A liquid not intended by God to be ingested by anything other than baby cows.

Another wave of lactose-induced nausea swept over her. She exhaled slowly, fighting it down. There couldn't be anything left in her stomach.

The wave lapped back into the ocean. Tsunami averted. She closed her eyes. And the phone rang.

Only one person could make her pick up the phone. And she was in no condition to talk to that one person. But if she didn't, Jay would think she was mad and she might never find out what she'd done wrong in the first place.

"Hello?"

"Hi."

Becky Melby

That voice. On most days it could calm whatever storm raged in her. On most days just the sound of his voice hung the sun in the sky. Not today. Not when she had no idea what he was going to say.

"Jay, my stomach's kind of acting up on me at the moment, so—"

"I'm sorry. Do you need anything? Chicken soup?"

Swallow. Breathe. Fight the wave. Please, no food. Just answers. "N-no. Thank you." She rose from the couch, shuffled to the kitchen chair. Closer to the bathroom.

"I walked out without saying good-bye last night. I was just . . . my head was spinning. It's a lot to take in, but I want you to know—"

"I'm the one who should be apologizing. I didn't really take into consideration how you were feeling. That was thoughtless. I shouldn't have put you in that position. I'm sure you felt trapped and then we didn't have a chance to talk. I'm sorry."

"Can I come over?"

Acid rose in her throat. The chair tipped as she lurched out of it. "Jay"—she darted toward the bathroom—"I'm really not feeling up to talking. Maybe—"

Chapter Three

*M*aybe *what*?

Jay scraped at the goo crusted on the oven door with more intensity than the job required. The strangled sound of her voice and the click of the phone disconnecting still blared in his head.

Lord, what do you want from me? What am I supposed to do? In his mind, he heard the *clack clack clack* of falling dominoes. He couldn't go to the elder board for advice. If he talked to some of them behind Bernard's back, they'd be obligated to act. First, by talking to Bethany. With kindness, of course. But what would be the outcome? She'd probably resign. Would it stop there? Jay would trust those men with his life. Godly men who gave wise counsel. Not a single one of them would gossip. Intentionally. But oh, how easy to let something slip. To forget for a split second in a conversation with a wife. One, unintended slip. One word.

Pregnant.

Clack. Clack. Clack.

Some would say she should be fired immediately. And how could a wayward woman play the role of the mother of Jesus in the pageant? No one would be cruel. Not intentionally. But, oh how easy to assume God has called you to be the Moral Police of Bethlehem Community.

Everyone would assume he was the father. So much for a lifetime of fighting temptation. Would anyone believe Jay had never so much as kissed her? And if he protested, claimed it was someone else, what would that say about either of them? They'd say he picked her up on the rebound. Or worse, that she'd two-timed him.

Would anyone go to Bethany and listen to the truth, whatever it was? And if the truth was ugly, what would that do to Christmas? What would happen to the girls she mentored?

What would happen to Ava?

Would they ask the pastor to leave quietly, to not make a scene at Christmas? But what about the scene he was supposed to make—the one where he played a man of honor who took the woman he loved to be his wife.

Lord, I can't tell anyone, can I? I can't do that to her. To us. To all of us. Not this week.

Eight days before Christmas is not the time to start a chain reaction.

❄

Elizabeth sat at the kitchen table, fingering the sticky note James had left on the bathroom mirror. She rested her chin on her hand. For six months she'd been going to the gym every Saturday morning and running at least three miles on the treadmill during the week. Now she couldn't summon the energy to walk to the sink. She chewed on a cracker as she stared at the remains of last night's less-than-celebration. Congealed gravy. Skin forming on leftover mousse. She could blame hormones for the queasiness, but the disappointment she'd awakened with wasn't caused by an increase in hCG.

She read the note again. *Call you if I can. Love you.*

"Do you?" She set her coffee cup on the yellow square. *Aren't there times in life when love means saying no to work?* If you could call it work.

He'd gotten the call from his boss a few bites into the pot roast and potatoes. He'd gone off to his gray-walled office and she'd picked at her food until the emotions of the day caught up with her. Exhausted, she'd fallen asleep on the couch before he got off the phone. James woke her with a kiss around ten. "Carl's kid had an appendicitis attack. I have to go to Keystone in the morning," he said. By the time she got out of the bathroom, he was snoring. This morning, he'd kissed her just after four and told her he was leaving.

Leaving for five days at a ski resort in Colorado. Keystone—a place that devoured cell phone signals like the Bermuda Triangle.

To his credit, he'd sounded frustrated that he had to "work" so far from home. Poor boy. At this moment he was drinking champagne in first class. For the next four days he'd be fawning over the siding and roofing company's best customers. And drinking more champagne. And skiing. While she went to work at the garden center Christmas zoo and nibbled soda crackers.

Elizabeth snapped her cracker in half, munched until her thoughts and stomach settled. She stared out into the living room. Christmas World, James called it. Three staggered-height fiber optic trees took up one corner, twinkling blue and white in time to music. *Jingle Bells. Here Comes Santa Claus. Have a Holly Jolly Christmas.* White LED candles surrounded a glass bowl filled with silver and white glass balls and lined the sill of the fourteen-foot tall arched window. Blue pillows embroidered with glittery snowflakes accented the white couch and loveseat. Last year she'd done red and gold.

There were advantages to managing a garden center that erupted in holiday glam from mid-October to the week after New

Year's. She had enough decorations in the basement to open her own store. Or become a personal decorator, which had once been her dream.

James wasn't big on Christmas. But that didn't stop her. Doesn't everyone need a reason for sparkle at least once a year?

She rose slowly from the kitchen table and ran water over the dishes. On the hill behind the house, sunlight glinted off freshly minted snowflakes. "See that, Joy? Perfect for sledding. Just enough slope to go fast, but not too fast." Two years from now, maybe three to be safe, she'd be bundling the little person now inside her in a snowsuit and mittens in preparation for an inaugural run down North Hill. Rosy cheeks. Giggles. Snow angels.

She leaned against the sink, wondering how it would feel to have a belly so big she'd have to turn sideways to reach the faucet. Wondering. It was what she'd wanted to do with James last night. Tucked under his arm, staring at the ceiling together but really looking into the future. Did James dream of tossing footballs, dancing with a tiny princess, carrying a sleepy toddler to bed?

Wondering would get her nowhere. She didn't need James to share her excitement. She needed paint. And empty boxes. Today she would take the dust-gathering trophies off the shelf and take down the navy curtains in the gray room.

Today she would make room for Joy.

Elizabeth stood before a wall of paint chips. She ran her fingertips across pastels so soft they could have been squares cut from a summer sky. Her index finger stopped on a bright green, the color of a Granny Smith apple. Delicious green. Was it a normal pregnancy thing to imagine you could taste colors, to want to dive into a pool of Cool Cucumber, Happy Honeydew, or Kickin' Kiwi and backstroke and summersault in a perfectly choreographed water ballet?

Green was life. And newness. And—her hand flew to her mouth—the way she felt at this very moment. She turned away, focused on a yellow that reminded her of being a little girl picking daisies in the field behind her grandmother's house. Yellow and white. Crisp, clean. Gender neutral. And unqueasy. A pallet that lent itself perfectly to future pops of pink or blue.

She slid two paint chips across the counter. The twenty-something in the electric blue Martin's Paint and Hardware smock with the pigtails and diamond stud in her nose picked it up. "Oooh." She pointed to the yellow. "Don't you just love this? It's like lemon chiffon. I just want to eat it." She reached for a pen. The move revealed a rounded profile.

A tiny shiver skittered up Elizabeth's arm. She leaned forward, lowered her voice. "Are you pregnant?"

Neatly shaped brows rose. Eyes narrowed. The smile flatlined.

Elizabeth's settled stomach unsettled. Heat surged from armpits to eyelashes. "I'm so sor—"

"Kidding!" The girl doubled as much as her swollen middle would allow then came up with a laughing gasp. "You should see your face!"

"I th-thought—"

"I know, right? I love doing that to people. Anyway, how much do you want of this scrumpdillyicious color?"

"A gallon. Satin, please. The same with the white."

"Whatcha gonna paint?"

"A nursery."

"So you're pregnant too?"

"No."

"Oh." Color bleached from around thick black mascara and heavy liner, giving the girl snowman eyes. "Oh man. Here I just—"

"Kidding!" Elizabeth sniggered and pointed. "You should see your face."

"I deserved that, didn't I? You got me." The girl toyed with the stud in her right eyebrow. "You're not doing the painting yourself, right? Not healthy breathing the fumes."

Why hadn't she thought of that? "No. My husband will do it. Should you be working here?"

"No. But I'm usually in back, handling inventory. We're just short-handed at the moment. If they don't hire somebody soon I'm going on strike. I have this recurring dream of having to mix paint between contractions."

"Paint chips would make great focal points."

She laughed. "Hadn't thought of that. When're you due?"

"June or July. I'll know more after my ultrasound."

"Cool beans. I'm due April 1."

"Do you know what you're having?"

The diamond chip in her nose sparkled as she nodded. "Nope. Maybe one of us is having a girl and the other a boy and they'll grow up and get hitched."

"I'll stop back in about 2030 so we can draw up the contract for an arranged marriage before they're old enough to date."

"You got a deal." She stuck out her hand. "I'm Shannon. You should know my name if I'm going to be your baby's mom-in-law."

"I'm Elizabeth. I look forward to planning a wedding with you, Shannon."

"One thing we can cross off our worry list, right?"

"Right."

"I'll get this mixed. Can't keep the other grandma of my future grandkids waiting."

❄

Elizabeth stomped snow off her boots and got into the car. Worry list. As if she didn't have a dozen—or two—of those. But this new list would trump the rest. After eighteen kidless years of marriage, what did they know about raising a child? There were books, of course. The girls at work bantered about them. *Say "Yes!" Parenting. Easy-Peasy Parenting. Spare the Rod. Conversational Parenting. Raising Kids by the Rules. Quiet Parenting.* What if they picked the wrong method? What if one little decision like not spanking led to a defiant two-year-old who turned into a rebellious sixteen-year-old who got in with the wrong crowd and ended up with a rap sheet longer than his or her arm? What if birthdays and Christmases were celebrated on separate sides of bullet proof glass and in every photograph above the mantle he or she was wearing orange? And what if he or she had red hair and looked awful in orange?

What if you have the next seven months to figure it all out?

Elizabeth took a slow breath. In through the nose, out through pursed lips. Her pulse returned to close to normal. For now, she'd start with *What to Expect When You're Expecting.*

A fine powdering of snow blew in swirls, danced on the windshield. As the shadows lengthened, shops glowed with little white lights. Giant wreaths with bright red bows hung from light posts. A year from now, she'd be Christmas shopping with a baby in her arms, singing carols as lullabies as they walked from store to store. The craft shop door opened just then and a woman came out, wrestling a stroller, diaper bag, wrapped box, and a foot-stomping toddler.

The carol-singing vision vanished. What if she didn't have the patience for being a mom? And James was used to order and quiet. And sleep.

One day at a time. She'd missed the call, the moment when James's confusion must have morphed into shock and then joy.

33

But they'd revisit it when he got back on Thursday. They'd sit by the fire and talk about the call and how to tell their parents. She'd seen the cutest idea on Pinterest—don't say a word, just hang a pair of baby shoes on the tree with her due date written on the bottom.

They'd talk about how to decorate the nursery. Did they want a new crib or a hand-me-down from one of their sisters?

James would opt for second hand. James would count the cost. He probably already knew what it cost to raise a child from birth to eighteen.

And what about college? Would they pay for four years? Or just half?

James was a planner. How would he handle it when his whiteboard of prioritized to-dos became a scribble board for a three-foot-tall munchkin, and his softball trophy shelves were filled with stuffed animals, and the sedate gray of the spare room was covered in lemon chiffon paint? What if they couldn't afford to remodel the kitchen and had to postpone their annual anniversary trip to Jamaica until 2030—right after she and the paint lady drew up the contract for the arranged marriage?

She tried to push the doubt aside, but it fought back like the venom-spitting dilophosaurus in Jurassic Park.

James didn't shift gears easily. What if he couldn't shift into daddy mode?

No. She wouldn't go there. Her dad always told her to counter the bad what ifs with good ones. What if her husband was really ecstatic and he'd just been in shock last night? Shock and distracted by the promotion. What if he walked in the house on Thursday, gathered her in his arms, said he couldn't wait to be a dad, and tipped her back in a dizzyingly romantic dip kiss?

Paint can in hand, she hummed the Blue Danube waltz as she sock skated across the kitchen tiles. She just wanted to try the paint—a tiny splotch in a hidden place. She set the can on the floor of the extra room, found a screwdriver, slid it into the groove around the lid and *fwop!* The cover flew across the room, landing upside down on the Green Back Packer jersey she'd promised to have framed for James.

The signed-by-Sterling Sharpe jersey he'd bought for five hundred and thirty-two dollars.

❄

Bethany woke around three in the afternoon with a genuine hunger pang. The lactose storm had subsided. She showered and ate a bowl of corn flakes. With almond milk—not the kind intended for bovine newborns. She sorted through yesterday's mail and checked her voicemail. How had she slept through two calls? One was from Lena, one of the girls she'd bailed on this morning, checking up on her. The other was Dr. Morganstein, CEO of H.I.S., Hands In Service.

She'd slept through a call from the man who'd hired her for the job of her dreams. Who does that? She tapped on the message. "Hi Bethany, this is Cameron Morganstein. Tried calling you yesterday too. Well, not to worry, you know what they say—if you want to get something done, ask a busy person. This confirms my conviction that you're the right person for the Inner City Short Term Missions Coordinator job. Should have a handier name for that, shouldn't we? Ring me Monday and we'll set up a time when you can come to St. Louis for orientation."

She grimaced. She should have heard the call. Her timing was off in everything. She'd applied for the job two weeks after moving back to Milwaukee and gotten the initial call a week later. They wanted her to replace the current coordinator who'd be retiring in January. Just days after she'd accepted the position, Sarah mentioned searching for a surrogate mother. How could she not offer to be the one to carry Dave and Sarah's child?

Sarah knew she'd be moving and said they'd work around it. Together, they'd found a doctor in St. Louis and had even visited the hospital where Bethany would deliver with Dave and Sarah—and Ava if all was going smoothly—at her side.

H.I.S. offered maternity leave, though she hadn't talked to Dr. Morganstein about the possibility. Sarah's health scares had stalled the process and there were just too many unknowns. So she hadn't put her life on hold. But now that this was actually happening, she wasn't sure about anything. About Jay, about uprooting Ava, about not allowing Sarah to be part of every stage of the pregnancy.

She devoted a few more minutes to self-condemnation, then got up, did some yoga stretches, and called Lena.

"Hi, Lena."

"Bethany! Are you okay? You sounded just awful!"

"All better. Hey, I'm free for the rest of the day if you and Destiny still want to meet."

"Great! I just talked to her and we're both bored crazy! Four o'clock at the coffee shop?"

Bethany looked at the clock. She'd have to leave in three minutes. But that's what you do when you're trying to talk Jesus to girls who talk in exclamation points. "I'll be there."

She drove past the church. Jay would be there putting finishing touches on his message. And praying. She'd witnessed it several times and hoped he didn't know. The first was by accident. After helping with a Saturday wedding, she remembered she'd left her camera on a pew in the balcony. The sanctuary was dark except for the dim lights around the roughhewn cross on the wall behind the platform. Something had stopped her when she put her hand on the light switch. A holy hush. She'd left the lights off and padded up the back stairs, the steps lit by an ethereal mosaic of color from the stained glass windows. When she reached the balcony, she heard something. Whispers. So low she couldn't make out the words. She peered down.

And that was the moment she fell in love.

Jay walked down the center aisle, stopping at each pew. Tilting his head, nodding, as if engaged in conversation. Which, she knew, he was—praying for Hank Spencer's heart problems, Max's marriage, little Jerome's earache, the businesses started by the residents of the Enterprise, and the babies due at Serenity. And when he finished, he walked up the steps and turned and began preaching to what he thought was an empty sanctuary.

He'd be there for hours, until he got it right. And by "right," Pastor Davidson didn't mean polished. He meant inspired by God.

She'd stop by the church after she met with the girls. If he was done, maybe they could talk. If not, she wouldn't mind hearing the Sunday-before-Christmas message twice.

And someday—if whatever he was mad about turned out to be some silly misunderstanding—maybe she would walk beside him instead of hiding in the balcony. And maybe, on Sunday mornings, she'd sit in the front pew.

Unless . . .

She was living six hours away.

Chapter Four

"Today we celebrate the beginning of a new chapter in many lives. Gathered here are people who share a common bond of love for a special baby boy whom you, together, have named Akanni Shakir Ellis-Price." Jay glanced at the adoptive parents, then offered a smile of encouragement to Alexandra, who moved to the rhythm of a silent lullaby as she rocked her child for the final time. Long black lashes rested on the baby's brown, pudgy cheeks. Tears graced the cheeks of the woman who had given birth to him and was about to make the greatest sacrifice of her life. Out of love.

"It's a big name for such a little one," Jay said, "but it is his parents' prayer that he will grow into this name which reflects his heritage, his future, and this moment. Akanni is a Nigerian name meaning 'our meeting brings gifts.' Shakir is also an African name, a name that means grateful. You have named this child together for the giving and the receiving. It is a tribute to Alexandra, the one who gave him life, and to Matthew and Melissa who will raise him to love our Lord and to always be grateful for this moment."

Alexandra placed the child of her womb into the waiting arms of Matthew Price. "I entrust my son to you. I have chosen you and Melissa because you are people of faith with hearts full of love. I know you will . . ."

As Alexandra continued in a surprisingly steady voice, Jay swiped at the dampness on his lashes. What would it be like to hold a child who became your own through a contract and a ceremony? Was Matthew afraid? Did he wonder if he had it in him to love this child the way he would love a son he had fathered? Jay had spent hours with Alexandra in the past eight months, listening and praying. He knew the heart of this woman and what it was costing her to give these people the greatest Christmas gift they would ever receive. But he'd only spent minutes with the birth parents who lived in Bayview. He'd spoken to their pastor and the adoption agency, but now he wished he'd had more time to talk to Matthew. To ask questions. To say, "How do you know you can be all this child needs?"

❄

When little Akanni and his entourage of new grandparents, aunts, uncles and cousins left and Jay had prayed with Alexandra until her tears had stopped, Jay sat alone in the front pew, staring at the cross that was lit from behind with a glow that always seemed like a visual reminder of the presence of God in this place. A swath of green satin draped over one arm of the cross. Green for new life. New birth.

A tall, spindly Christmas tree filled a place of honor to the right of the cross. An artificial tree worthy of Charlie Brown. Three years ago, Jay had suggested putting on an outdoor nativity in front of the church. The entire elder board told him he was nuts. "They won't come to us. We have to take the message to them," he'd argued.

It was a no go. Until Yolanda got wind of the idea. No one who wanted to live to tell about it said no to Yolanda. And so it came to pass that on the night before Christmas Eve, the artificial tree covered in white lights stood guard over angels in white sheets and fuzzy earmuffs and shepherds in their fathers' bathrobes. Yolanda sang "Silent Night" while a girl with a blue bath towel over her head rocked a bundle of blankets.

Silent Night. Holy Night.

Until the tree tipped over. Again. After Jay said a word a pastor should never say, he moved the actors five feet to the left to make room for the tree on the relatively level corner where two sidewalks converged. When everyone found their new places and Mary found her rocking rhythm once again, Yolanda began to sing.

Silent Night. Holy Night.

Until the car with the pounding rap music and roaring engine careened around the corner, bounced over the curb, and slammed into the tree. The tree Jay had moved to the exact spot where, five minutes earlier, Mary sat rocking her blanket bundle and children in bathrobes sang Silent Night.

And so the tree, wounded and broken, but covered in new lights, now reigned over Christmas. The sacrificial tree that took the punishment in their place. A sermon in itself.

Jay stood, walked down the aisle, stopping to touch the carved end of each pew, praying over each wounded person who would fill it. And the ones who, tomorrow morning, would fight the Voice that invited them to walk through the peeling-red-paint doors.

In the middle of the sanctuary, he stopped with his hand on one of the worn wooden pews and looked up at the arched stained glass window. Jesus kneeling in the Garden of Gethsemane. The window not only depicted the hours before the greatest miracle ever witnessed—the window *was* a miracle.

Bethlehem Community Church had been a landmark since 1867. Two years after the Civil War ended. How had that long-ago, war-weary congregation come up with the money to build a solid brick church and crown it with a twelve-foot-tall stained glass window imported from France?

But that was not the miracle.

The miracle was that, as decades passed and the affluent neighborhood that grew up around the church at the end of the nineteenth and early twentieth century crumbled physically and morally through the years, the window still *was*.

Until the past few years, it was not uncommon for the deacons to be called in the middle of the night to board up a broken window. Once, Jay had walked in and found a man sleeping on the floor in what the old timers called the "overflow" room. But things were changing. Because the Enterprise offered inexpensive housing to entrepreneurs who wanted to start businesses in Holly Park, the neighborhood surrounding the green space named in honor of Buddy Holly, whose Winter Dance Party Tour began with a concert in Milwaukee in January of 1959 and ended tragically with a plane crash three weeks later.

Because of the Enterprise, the crack house across the street became Serenity, a haven for single moms, and Square Peg, a clothing boutique, repurposed what had once been a tavern. A run-down auto parts store was bought by Max Nowicki, who did custom motorcycle painting, and Vienna Marshal and her college age daughter bought a liquor store and were almost ready to start selling vitamins and organic produce.

Every Saturday, May through October, Bethlehem members gave their time and talents to paint and mow and fix roofs and plant flowers. As they loved on people, Sunday attendance increased. Maybe he would yet see the day when, as it had been back in the thirties and forties, the main sanctuary would be too small and the accordion doors would need to be opened to allow worship to overflow into the side room.

Jay stared up at the serene face of Jesus.

Over the years, in the midst of the whiskey and the cocaine and the brawls and the broken glass and broken lives, Jesus kneeled in the garden. Unbroken.

Lord, you knew what was coming. You knew the soul-shattering rejection and searing pain awaiting you. And yet you didn't turn away. Give me a little bit of that. Just a tiny shard of the kind of love that doesn't waver in the face of jeering and humiliation.

"Jay?"

She stood before him. For a second he thought he was witnessing another miracle. A vision of Bethany just at the moment he'd prayed.

"Jay? Are you okay?"

Once again, he blinked as if emerging from a dream. "I'm fine. The question is, how are you?" And a million other hows. *How are you feeling? How far along are you? How are we going to make this work?*

"I'm great. Slept all morning and I'm back to normal."

A new normal, maybe. How many mornings would she need to sleep through to feel normal for the rest of the day? "Good."

"I wasn't sure you'd accepted my apology. I had to see your face." She smiled and took a few steps closer.

Three feet and a million questions separated them, but all Jay could think of was holding her. And so he did. He closed the gap and wrapped his arms around her. "I forgive you. And I don't even need to know—"

"Go tell it on the mountain, over the hills and *whoops!*" Yolanda, wearing a faux fur coat that made her look like Baloo from Jungle Book, swept into the sanctuary and rocked the back pew as she came to a skidding halt. "Oh my, my. Pretend I was never here. I am so sorry. Here I go. Walking out. Leaving now." She stepped backwards, floor groaning beneath her, white teeth gleaming in a grin on the verge of exploding. "Rewind. Go on back to whatev—"

"Yolanda." Bethany had already eased out of his arms. "We were just . . . talking. Do you need something?"

"Nothing that can't wait. Nothing as important as what—"

A crash sounded from the side room. And then the distinct sound of change rolling across the floor. A lot of change. Yolanda gasped. "Shoot! I didn't lock the door behind me." A wide hand with rings worn over gold gloves slid into a faux fur pocket and pulled out a pistol.

"Yolanda!" Jay raised both hands as if she were pointing it at him. "This is a church. Put that thing away!"

"Fine. You go be brave, Super Pastor. But someone's stealing the cash box from the fundraiser and I'm keepin' my hand on this thing."

Jay shook his head and strode past her—walking like a super pastor, though his insides were beginning to quiver a bit. Maybe he should have grabbed the gun.

A shepherd's crook leaned against the basement railing. He snatched it and held it up, ready to strike. As he stealthily turned the corner into the overflow room, something rolled across the floor. A roll of quarters. He squared his shoulders and faced the thief—a giant, grinning man in a plaid coat and snow-dusted pony tail. With a chicken in his backpack.

❄

"Sorry we startled you." The man stood, hands in the air, in front of a tower of spice boxes from the Serenity fundraiser.

"We?" Jay looked from side to side, quickly turning his vigilance back on the man.

"Esther and I. She knocked that box down. I think she smelled something tasty in here." He nodded toward the shepherds' crook. "Guess you thought I was robbing the place."

Jay kept his weapon at the ready. "Can we help you, sir?"

Yolanda, who was blocking Bethany with one massive arm, kept her gun hand in her pocket. "Looks like he was helpin' himself," she muttered. "Gotta be over a hundred bucks in that box."

"He doesn't look too dangerous," Bethany whispered back. "Maybe he just needed some thyme and sage for his chicken dinner."

"That's disgusting."

"I was looking for the church office. Thought I might offer my services."

The shepherd's crook lowered several inches. "Why don't you have a seat."

"Okay if I put my hands down?" He nodded toward the crook. "Don't want to make any fast moves with that thing pointed at me."

Jay leaned the crook against a chair and extended his hand. "Jay Davidson. I'm the pastor here." Jay motioned toward the women. "This is Yolanda Holt, my body guard who doubles as our music director, and Bethany Schmidt, the person you'd have to answer to if you were stealing our fundraiser money."

"Clarence Hoover." The man engulfed Jay's hand in his. "Just call me Hoover. And this is Esther." He introduced his chicken with a note of pride and a hint of Irish brogue. "She fell off a truck. Saved her life, I did."

"She's"—Bethany searched for a complimentary chicken adjective—"pretty."

"That she is." Hoover lowered the chicken to the floor, opened a granola bar, crushed it, and put the crumbs on the floor. Then he sat in the chair Jay offered him.

Jay pulled a chair closer to Hoover. "What brings you to our part of town?"

"Just passing through. I've heard good things about Bethlehem Community Church. Thought I'd check it out."

Jay leaned back against the back of the chair. "Glad you stopped by. We're usually a bit more welcoming to strangers. Anything in particular you want to know?"

"I'm looking for some temp work. Any chance you need a bit of help around here?"

Jay gave a rueful laugh. "Help, we need. But we can't pay."

Bethany pulled up a chair. "What kind of job are you looking for?"

"Well, what do you need? I'm a carpenter by trade, but I'm willing to do just about anything."

"How long will you be in town?"

"Depends on the work I find."

"Where are you staying?"

"Haven't figured that out yet."

Jay turned to Bethany. "Is the apartment open?"

She nodded. "George moved out two days ago."

"Well, Mr. Hoover, we can offer you a place to live for thirty days and can help you find a job."

Bethany stared at Jay. He was not following protocol. What about the application and background check? The guy hadn't answered a single question with a real answer. Maybe he had been raiding the cash box. Who knows what he might be up to. And what about the chicken? Sure, they didn't have any rules against animals at the Enterprise, but shouldn't there be a rule against critters that didn't walk on a leash or use a litter box? *Jay, what are you thinking?*

But Jay was a good judge of character—in a church that was in no short supply of characters.

But they didn't have a chicken yet.

No point protesting. Mr. Hoover and his feathered friend were already invited to move in. She smiled at the man. "There are ten of us living in the building next door and six across the street. We'll all be gathering for a communal meal on Christmas

45

Becky Melby

Day. Ham, turkey, sweet potatoes, pie, and a whole lot more. Happy to have you join us if you don't have other plans."

"No other plans, thank you, ma'am. But I won't be staying long unless I can earn my keep."

"Don't worry. We'll keep you busy." Jay stood. "Let's go look at that apartment." As they walked out, he said, "Seems only fitting a church called Bethlehem would welcome an itinerant carpenter at Christmastime."

❄

Chapter Five

E lizabeth scraped at the ring of yellow paint with a plastic spoon. She was stuck on the first of five recommended steps: 1. Blot up or scrape off excess paint. 2. Rinse the spot in running water to flush. 3. Treat the spot with equal parts dishwashing liquid and warm water. 4. Pre-treat the spot with commercial stain remover. 5. Wash as you would normally.

She couldn't bring herself to attempt Step 2, putting water on the jersey that was never washed after Sterling Sharpe wore it for a winning touchdown in 1994. James and his dad were sitting in Row 4 in the end zone at Lambeau Field that night—one of very few positive father-son moments in his life. James had been searching online for this jersey for the past five years.

Washing number 84 wasn't an option. It might take the paint out, but it would also remove the grass stain on the shoulder that even the manager of a garden center couldn't replicate in December in Wisconsin. Frozen tundra didn't leave a green stain. *Lord, help*. She wasn't a praying person, but she was desperate.

She tried another site. This one suggested using dry cleaning solvent. All out of that.

The phone rang and she jolted upright. Her pulse banged in her ears as she picked up the phone. A guilty pulse. "James. Hi! I didn't think you'd be able to call."

"Hey, babe. How—?" His voice echoed then faded away.

"I didn't get all that. I'm good. You?"

"Great. Hooked up with an old"—echo, fade—"Chris Wilson. And . . .Dad . . . news."

"Really?" Wasn't that something they should do together? So much for baby shoes on the tree. She blinked back the sting of tears. She could still do that for her parents. "What did he say?"

". . . know my dad. Had to . . . not measuring up. He said, '. . . about time!'" James laughed. The kind of laugh she'd heard often over the years—the one he used to cover the hurt.

"Did you talk to your mom?" Alanna Schmidt was her husband's polar opposite. She'd rejoice with them. "Is she excited about the baby?"

"Maybe what? You're breaking . . ."

She repeated the question.

". . . take you to Carnevor for filet . . ."

The thought of a medium rare steak swimming in juice the way she usually loved it made her salivary glands revolt. "That would be nice." Swallow. Breathe.

"Hey . . . waiting for me. . . .you back later?"

"Sure. We'll be right here waiting."

"We?" He laughed. "You . . . party while I'm gone? Talk to you—"

No good-bye. No "I love you." Elizabeth stared out at the snow, feeling empty and alone.

The blank phone screen taunted her. She had to talk to someone. Someone who would understand—about pregnancy and paint stains.

Three swipes and a click brought Martin's Paint and Hardware to her fingertips.

❄

Jay walked out of Hoover's apartment to find Bethany waiting for him in the hallway. The rustic smell of the beef stew and cornbread she'd warmed for their new tenant mingled with the scent of her perfume. Earthy, welcoming. Homey.

Growing up in the foster care system, he'd created an imaginary home and family—a mind space he could retreat to when, once again, he was shuffled off to another home that never felt like one. In his pretend world he lived in a farmhouse, tall and white with a red front door. It sat in the middle of a massive yard with giant trees. In his day dreams he had a dog and a tree house and a tire swing. And lots of brothers and sisters.

Strange that after a lifetime of longing for a place to call home and people to call family, he'd finally found it in the middle of the city in an old converted school populated by eccentric, artsy people who had nothing in common. Nothing but a love for Jesus and His kids.

Bethany handed him a travel mug with a Chicago Bears logo. "Starbeth's Christmas special," she said. "Peppermint mocha."

He thanked her without a snide remark about her football loyalties. It took all of his waning self-control to keep from sealing his gratitude with a kiss.

"Is he settling in?"

"Yeah. Only had a small duffle. Strange guy, huh?"

"I like him. Them."

"So that's what I have to do to get your attention? Buy a chicken?"

She laughed and he echoed. It felt good to pretend they were just two singles flirting in the hallway.

"Feel like taking a walk?" Any other time he might have just said "Want to" instead of "Feel like."

"Sure." The smile that had framed a laugh faded. "We need to talk."

When they reached the corner, he took her elbow with one hand and put his other arm around her waist. "Careful now."

They walked and sipped in silence until after they crossed the street. Thin wisps of snow swirled around their feet. White lights on wreaths that looked saggy and bedraggled in the daylight glowed against a navy sky. A bluesy version of "Deck the Halls" streamed through the open door of the Green Goose tavern. Jay took a breath intended to be calming. "Before we talk about anything else, I need to know something."

"About what?" Hash marks formed between her eyebrows.

"I need to know if"—he took a chance on the name—"Peter is . . ." He stalled, not sure how he wanted to phrase it. He needed to know more than just the facts of the baby's paternity. He had to know if she was still in any kind of relationship with him.

"Peter? Is that it? Jay, I told you that was over. I was a fool to fall for someone who had so little respect for me and absolutely no interest in being a husband or a father. He talked the talk but it was all a lie. I have no feelings for him, Jay. None. Well, no good ones anyway. He is out of the picture. Completely. I don't know what else I can do to make you believe that." She stopped then bent and set her cup on the sidewalk. "Except maybe this." Her lips met his.

Willpower evaporated, blowing away like the snow at their feet. He grabbed her by the shoulders and surrendered to her kiss.

❄

The sidewalk tilted beneath Bethany's feet like the deck of a tugboat in twenty foot waves. The kiss felt like home and tasted like heaven, but what had she done? She gazed up at eyes that reflected the tavern's flashing OPEN sign. Open. Like the can of worms she'd just set free.

Neither of them were the type to say a kiss was just a kiss. Jay would read it as a promise. A promise she couldn't give until she'd told him everything.

His smile outshined all the neon in the Green Goose window. Gloved fingertips brushed the hair from her cheek. "Hungry?"

Her stomach lurched at the thought of the conversation they needed to have. Since yesterday afternoon she'd had so many conversations with him in her head. In some, he hugged her, pride shining in his eyes. "I'm so proud of you, Bethany. What a selfless act of love. Of course I'll be by your side through it all." And then there were the ones where he said, "In vitro is just messing with God's plan. It's a lack of faith on your sister's part. How could you possibly be involved in that?" Or worse: "You don't actually think I'm going to put my life on hold while you fulfill someone else's dreams, do you?"

If she didn't blurt it out soon she'd go crazy. But who broke news like this just days before Christmas? Jay had to preach tomorrow and on Christmas Day. She couldn't scramble his brain like that. She took a deep breath. She wouldn't do that to him. "I'm starving."

Whatever it took, from this moment until sometime after Christmas, she'd keep things light. "How about sushi?"

Jay's tongue stretched out, the tip nearly touching his chin. He gripped his throat with both hands, coughed and staggered.

Bethany rolled her eyes. Something Misty had said yesterday came to mind. *This is rare even for you.* "Fine. I give. You're such a chicken."

"Pizza?"

She grabbed her throat and wretched. Quite realistic since her recent practice.

"Fine. Something dairy- and seaweed-free. Cheeseless burgers." He pointed up the street, took a step, then stopped. "How can you be sure you're getting enough calcium? Do you take those pink vitamins?"

She tipped her head to one side. "You're worried about my calcium intake."

"Yes. Aren't you?"

She laughed. "No. I take supplements and eat lots of green leafy veggies. And sardines with bones."

His face twisted in a look of revulsion. "You can still eat those things?"

"Still? I've loved sardines since I was a little kid."

"Okay." He gave a sigh that clearly said she was crazy. "And for the record, I am not a chicken. I am ichthyophobic."

"Is it contagious?"

"It means I have a healthy fear of eating raw fish."

"Then what's your excuse for zucchini?" She wrinkled her nose at him, then quickly relaxed it back to normal. On their last date he'd told her that was cute. No more cute. No more coy. And definitely no more kissing. Until after she told him everything, they were simply friends.

"I can't spell it." He opened the door to Barbie's Burger Bar and Bethany stepped inside, careful to leave as much space between them as the door would allow.

She was still perusing the menu when she felt his stare. She looked up into eyes that searched her like a heat-seeking missile. She had to disarm him and keep him disarmed through a triple bacon, Swiss, and mushroom burger with ranch fries. They'd had enough pre-dating work lunches together to know what he'd order in any of the restaurants within a five block radius. "Feeling good about tomorrow's message?"

"I don't know. I was. Now I'm not so sure."

"Why?"

"It's called 'Are You Ready for Bethlehem?'"

"Great title."

"Yeah. But I'm beginning to question whether I'm the right person to deliver it. I'm trying to get into Joseph and Mary's heads. What would it be like to suddenly get a call saying the woman you loved is pregnant and it's not your child but you're supposed to love it anyway?"

His gaze bore into her, challenging a response. What was he getting at? Was this about Ava? Hadn't they already talked this through? On their first date she'd made it clear she had no interest in recreational dating. She didn't have that luxury. "I'm a thirty-one-year-old mom who's made a ton of mistakes," she'd said. "The one thing I am going to do right, no matter what the cost, is protect my daughter." He'd smiled as if she amused him and then he'd made her cry. "Bethany," he'd said, "I would never have asked you out if I hadn't prayed like crazy and spent enough time around Ava to know. . . ." He hadn't finished the sentence, but she'd filled in the blanks in her mind. *To know I could love you both.*

But now, with him burning holes in her with that thousand-watt stare, she wasn't so sure. She took a deep breath, but blew it out when their server approached.

Jay seemed a bit more relaxed after they ordered and it had given her time to think how to answer. "I can't imagine what Joseph was thinking. No one would have blamed him for walking away." *There, I just gave you an out. Take it now if you need to, just please don't jerk me around.* If he was telling her he couldn't handle the talk and gossip of courting a woman who'd gotten pregnant out of wedlock, it would save her the anxiety of broaching the subject of surrogacy. And a month from now she'd be in St. Louis.

His hand slid across the table, fingertips touching hers. "But he loved her."

It was her turn at the laser stare. She'd told him everything. He knew about Ava's father. Three months after he'd proposed, Rick died in basic training. Heart valve defect they'd said. No idea why doctors hadn't caught it earlier. He never knew she was pregnant. She was saving the surprise for his graduation day.

There had been no one for eight years, and then Peter walked into their lives with all the right words. She'd fallen hard. So had Ava. But a year later, there was no talk of marriage so she'd brought it up. A week after that he had a job offer in Los Angeles. She looked away from Jay. "Sometimes love isn't enough."

Jay sighed. His shoulders slumped. "Do you think it was enough for Mary? Did she really love him?"

"A man who would face that kind of shame for you . . . yeah, I think she loved him."

"He was only human." He rolled the edge of his napkin. "There were probably times he didn't feel up to the task. Maybe he wondered if he'd really talked to an angel or if he'd only imagined it."

"She probably had those thoughts too. At least until she felt the baby move." Bethany put her hand on her belly, part illustration, part remembering. Part thinking ahead. Could she do this again? Go through a pregnancy without the support of a man? Sarah and Dave would be there for her. Dad would treat her like she was a porcelain doll. But it wasn't the same. And this time, though she couldn't imagine ever regretting the decision to give her sister the child she never thought she'd have, Bethany would be left with empty arms. "I think Mary must have felt very alone at times. I think she must have wondered if Joseph really loved her or if he was only doing the right thing."

Jay's hand slid over hers. His mouth curved in the sweetest of smiles. "But they made it work, didn't they?"

She gave her best imitation of a smile. "I suppose they did."

But wait until you hear the rest.

Jay wouldn't just be faced with fathering a child he hadn't fathered. Was he the kind of man who could support her through the pregnancy and birth of a child that wasn't his . . . *or* hers? A child he *couldn't* father?

It would take a real present-day Gabriel to make that happen.

Chapter Six

"*M*orning." Bethany slid into their usual pew next to her father and kissed his cheek.

He grabbed her hand and squeezed it. His eyes shimmered. He blinked hard and his Adam's apple dipped and rose. "Morning, sweetie," his whispered, voice rough and low.

Bethany's chest tightened. "What's wrong?"

"Sarah and Dave stopped by the house last night." He squeezed her fingers. "Thank you." A tear slid down his cheek. Bernard Schmidt wasn't a crying man.

"She would have done it for me."

"I know." He swiped his chin. "Someone raised my girls right." He smiled and pointed upward. He knew that "someone" wasn't him. The first forty years of his life had been spent gambling, carousing, drinking, and neglecting his family. And then, on the night of her thirteenth birthday, he'd knelt beside her bed and asked her forgiveness and told her about Jesus.

Eight years passed before those words meant anything to her. By then her mother had died from an overdose and Bethany was pregnant and homeless and considering ending her life. Instead, she went home. And learned the story of the prodigal son whose father opened his arms and welcomed him back applied to girls too. She'd stayed home for two years, then moved to Chicago to work at a Bible college.

Bethany squeezed back and nodded. "Someone raised us *all* right."

"I had another visitor last night."

"Who?"

"Jay."

Bethany swallowed reflexively. "Oh? Church business?"

"Nope. This was personal."

"Oh? About what?"

He pressed his shoulder into hers and winked. "Personal stuff."

Misty tiptoed into the pew next to Bethany. "Guess what?" Misty rarely bothered with mundane words like Hi and Goodbye. "I got tickets to the Nutcracker for you and me and Ava for Thursday night."

"How'd you do that? I thought they were . . . sold out." The last two words trailed off as Jay walked in the side door and took his place in the front row. Before sitting, he turned and caught her eye. Just a hint of a smile, but it snared her like Spiderman's web.

Seven days. She only had to hold it together for one week. A week that included working together and a rehearsal with an ogling cast snickering and giggling when she and Jay held hands over the manger and sang "You and I." *You and I are only human. We can't do this on our own. But you and I are not alone. God will guide us, help us, change us. God will change us, you and I.*

"Connections."

"Huh?"

Misty waved a hand in front of Bethany's face. "I've got connections. I know people. But we have to pray Jocelyn doesn't go into labor that night."

"Oh. Tickets. Right."

"You okay?"

Not even close. She smiled. "Couldn't be better," she lied, as she stared at the back of Jay's neck. *We can't do this on our own.*

But would there even be a "we"?

❄

"Are You Ready for Bethlehem? Are we ready to welcome the baby who was Jesus Christ come to earth in human form?" Jay moved away from the podium that separated him from the congregation. He'd felt separate his whole life. No more. He stepped off the platform and stared out at a sanctuary more than half full. When he'd come here as a young, green associate pastor, twenty-two people were scattered throughout this room on a Sunday morning. It wasn't about numbers, but the filled pews were evidence God was doing something here.

"In preparing for my role as Joseph in our Christmas program, I've done some soul searching. I've tried to envision Joseph's world: Small town carpenter just going about his day like he always did, maybe whistling to himself, probably imagining married life, thinking about the dark-eyed girl he'd soon call his wife. Like most young men who think their future is theirs to plan, he may have decided how many kids they'd have. The boys would be just like him. The girls like Mary. He could imagine working side-by-side with his sons, sons who'd grow up to be just like their daddy."

A few nods and smiles showed they were listening.

"*And then* . . . How many of you have had your perfect plans changed by an 'and then'?" Most of the people raised their hands, a few laughed. He chanced a look at Bethany and caught her shoulders lowering and eyes closing.

"We don't know if Joseph was a devout man. We can assume he was. A man who did his best to follow God's law. But nothing had prepared him for a visitor from heaven." He gestured at one of the side windows. Two of the nine panes had been replaced

57

with frosted glass, but enough of the original stained glass remained to show the artist's rendition of a winged angel, delicate hands folded in repose, pale effeminate face tilted to one side.

"Now I'm no expert and I've had no personal experience, but from what I gather from scripture, angels are not pretty, wimpy-looking beings. Nor are they loveable bumblers like"—a bizarre thought drew his attention like a circling mosquito—"the angel in *It's a Wonderful Life*. And while we're on that—angels don't have to earn their wings, so every time a bell rings, it probably just means supper's ready."

He loved the laughter of these people, loved that he could put smiles on faces that maybe hadn't smiled in the seven days since they'd last met. If it took an occasional rabbit trail to accomplish that, he was pretty sure the Lord was good with it.

"Daniel talks about encountering a being with a face like lightning, eyes like flaming torches, arms and legs gleaming like bronze, and a voice like the sound of a multitude. So most likely the angel who appeared to Joseph in a dream didn't even remotely resemble the figurines we hang on our Christmas trees. These guys are God's warriors. They're soldiers. That's why we chose Dante over here to be our Gabriel. We needed a guy nobody would mess with."

Laughter bounced off the arched ceiling. And then another sound joined in. A muffled *bawk!*

Hoover sat nodding emphatically in an aisle seat. Esther poked out of his jacket, bobbing her head in time with his.

"When Joseph looked up from his sleeping mat and into the glowing eyes of—"

Bawk-bawk-BAWK! Esther leapt from Hoover's knee and flew into the aisle. A woman in the back screamed, a baby cried, and three-year-old Jerome, who lived at Serenity with his mom, jumped up and down in his pew clapping his hands. Esther flapped back.

"Well, folks, I learned a long time ago to go with the flow."
Jay motioned to Hoover.

"Would you mind coming up here, so everyone can meet you
two?"

❄

Bethany cringed. What was Jay doing? Interruptions were
nothing new in this group, but it wasn't like Jay to put someone
on the spot until he knew they wouldn't mind.

"With pleasure." Hoover scooped up Esther and walked to
the front.

"Hoover here just moved into the Enterprise yesterday. I've
only spent a little time with him, but he's one of those people you
feel like you've known forever. And because we're a body that
takes care of each other, if you know of anyone looking to hire a
jack of all trades, he's eager to find work." Jay stepped back and
nodded.

"Thank you. Hoping to have a face-to-face with each one of
you in the very near future. This is my buddy Esther. She's
harmless as a dove, just a mite bigger." He picked up Esther's
foot and waved. The congregation clapped a welcome.

"I've popped in on many a church and rarely do I find people
so warm and welcoming. Bethlehem Community truly practices
hospitality." He put a huge hand on Jay's shoulder. "Mind if I
steal your next line, pastor?"

"Go right ahead."

"As angels so often do, the first thing that big guy did was tell
Joseph not to be afraid. Good words, huh? I wonder if there might
be some people here this morning who need to hear that."

Bethany had a feeling every person in the room thought he
was looking directly at them. Or into them. "No matter what
you're dealing with now or what happens next"—Hoover
stretched out his hand as if in benediction—"do not be afraid."

❄

Was it her imagination, or did Jay's energy seem to lag after Hoover sat down? He usually spoke with such humble conviction. Now, some of the sentences she was sure he'd written as statements were posed as questions.

"Is God calling us this week to say yes to something we can't accomplish in our own strength? Is he asking us—each of us individually and Bethlehem Community as a whole—to trust him to lead us out of what is familiar and comfortable? How often do we rationalize when we feel the Holy Spirit giving a gentle push? 'This can't be from God,' we say, "because . . .' Imagine how Mary could have filled in that blank. 'This can't be from God because I'm too young, I'm not married, what would people think, what will Joseph say? She did ask for clarification. 'How can this be?' And when the angel told her the Holy Spirit would come upon her and the power of the Most High would overshadow her and the Holy One she would give birth to would be called the Lord's Servant, she didn't balk." He laughed, transforming to more of his usual demeanor. "Unlike Esther, she didn't *bawk*."

When the groans had died down, he continued. "Mary didn't argue or offer a Plan B. She said, 'I am the Lord's servant. May it be to me as you have said.' And when Gabriel appeared to Joseph in a dream, he responded the same way. Scripture says simply, 'When Joseph woke up, he did what the angel of the Lord had commanded.'

"I don't know about you, but I can see how this would play out in my life." He looked toward the angel window. "I'd be like, 'Whoa, hold on a sec. I've got a plan. Didn't you read the Life Mapping book? I've got things to do, places to go, people to meet. Maybe in a few years. How about that, Gabe? You come back when I'm like fifty and I've checked off everything on my bucket list. Then we'll talk. Deal?'

"Where would we all be if Joseph had said, 'No way'? And where do we end up when we refuse to listen to God's commands?" Jay walked down the middle aisle. "I, for one, want to wake up and do what the Lord commands."

Bethany's pulse skittered as his gaze rested on her.

He gave just the faintest smile. "I want to be a Joseph."

Chapter Seven

"Reorder the skinny wood snowmen, Margie. A dozen. Tell them to overnight them." Elizabeth thanked the girl who'd answered the office phone as she scanned a wall of blue ornaments. They didn't always group them by color, but this year it had just seemed right. There was that color thing again—skewing her judgement long before she was aware of it. Her customers would never know they were browsing hormone-driven displays.

She nodded her approval at the coppers and browns across the aisle. A giant ball covered in thick glitter—bronze and brown and gold—captured her senses. She motioned to the girl restocking glass candy canes in the red section. "Kelsey, what would you think about decorating that ten-foot balsam around this?" She held up the ball.

"Perf. Can I?"

Elizabeth gritted her teeth and gave the go ahead. Millennials. Kelsey was one of her best employees, but deciphering her vocabulary required a dictionary update every week. "I'm meeting someone next door at one. You're in charge."

"Got it."

"Is that wise?" Nora, her disheveled boss, appeared out of nowhere. Nora, the rain cloud in a job she could love if she felt respected.

"She's proven herself."

Nora *tsk*ed and walked away. It wasn't a requirement of her job to tell her boss her sweater was buttoned wrong, was it?

At the coffee shop she ordered a large coffee with cream and sugar. No more artificial sweeteners. She'd spent Sunday curled in a chair by the fiber optic trees, staring out at the snow and reading up on dos and don'ts. What would James say when he came home to a pantry void of cheese puffs and beef sticks? How many times had she jokingly used the line from Elf, "You smell like beef and cheese"? She swallowed hard against the bile creeping up her throat. There would be none of that this year. He'd be snacking on fresh fruit and raw organic cheese—but only the kind that didn't smell like dirty feet or baby spit-up.

She found a round table for two near a window. Along with tasting colors, she was craving light. Open spaces. Was that normal? She'd find out in a minute. A bell above the door jingled and Shannon walked in, spotted her and waved, then walked up to the counter. Elizabeth studied her. An unlikely choice of friend. She had to be at least a decade and a half younger and she had a diamond stud in her nose and a hummingbird tattooed on her wrist. Well, if this turned awkward and they had nothing in common, she'd just have to buy her paint at Home Depot and their paths would never cross again.

Shannon walked up, set her cup down, and gave Elizabeth a quick hug. "Hi. Whatcha drinking?"

"Holiday Blend. You?"

"Peppermint mocha. I know I shouldn't. Supposed to be watching my sugar. But a girl's gotta splurge once in a while, right?"

So far, it appeared they followed the same life philosophy. "Right."

"How's the jersey?"

"Back to new—or old—thanks to your expertise. Hairspray worked like a charm."

"Going to tell your hubby?"

Elizabeth took the cover off her coffee. "Someday."

"Is he the big scary construction kind or the quiet computer geek kind?"

Elizabeth laughed. "Kind of in between. He works for a roofing and siding company. He used to do the work, now he just sells the stuff."

"Is he excited about the baby?"

"I'm . . . not sure." She explained the unplanned trip to Colorado. "So you're five months. How are you feeling?"

Years ago, she'd stopped posing that question to the pregnant girls at the store. Their talk of heartburn and back aches and swollen ankles had only made her feel bad. More than once she'd gone into the restroom to cry because she didn't have puffy ankles and she'd never know what a Braxton-Hicks contraction felt like. But now, she devoured every word.

They'd been talking for half an hour when Shannon's phone dinged. She picked it up. "Sorry. Sounds strange that I'm on call at a paint store, but I work for my in-laws." Shannon read the text and smiled as she tapped an answer. She looked up at Elizabeth. "My mother-in-law is sending someone here for me to interview."

"Yay. Maybe you can get off your feet once in a while."

The phone dinged again. Shannon's mouth twisted to one side. "Weird. Read this." She handed the phone to Elizabeth.

Don't judge on appearance. Seems like a good guy. Don't let the chicken scare you.

❄

Jay had outlined his Sunday message in his head, but there were things he wanted to say that were still squishing around in his brain without form or substance. A gelatinous ooze of impressions and feelings he couldn't press into word molds.

He strode across the area rug in his living room, then stopped and listened. Sometimes, if he was very quiet and the goth guy next door was listening to *Darkness Falls Upon This Christmas* on his headphones instead of letting carols sung as dirges seep into the hallway, he could hear Bethany's key fitting into the lock and the door handle bumping into the wall as she came in with her arms full. The girl always had her arms full.

He glanced at the clock. She was supposed to quit work at four, but he knew she wouldn't this week. She'd tidy up her desk then head down to the basement to work on decorations for Sunday. Such as they were. And then she'd busy herself folding napkins that were just fine unfolded.

This was supposed to be his day off. He should be doing something fun. Or finishing his Christmas shopping. He still hadn't figured out what to get Bethany. He was actually glad he hadn't gotten the necklace he'd looked at online. Or the restaurant gift card. Or the purse he'd caught her staring at in Square Peg's shop window. He needed something meaningful. But what?

He walked the perimeter of the braided rug one more time, stopping at the clay nativity set Ava had made for him last year. Last year she'd spent Christmas vacation with Bethany's father. That kid. Did she know she'd carved out a permanent place in his heart?

He picked up the manger. She'd used the end of a paper clip to etch wood grain in the brown clay, then filled it with gold tinsel. "It's empty because the baby isn't born yet," she'd said. And then, on Christmas Eve, she'd given him a tiny bundle of tissue paper and tape. Inside, a perfect little clay baby. "I'll take it back next week and give it to you every year, okay?"

"You better. Can't leave the manger empty. That would be a real game changer."

She laughed. "We'd have to cancel Christmas."

"And I'd be out of a job."

He fingered a strand of gold. *Can't leave the manger empty. We'd have to cancel Christmas.* He paused, held it up to the light. "That's it." He pointed at the ceiling. "Knew you'd come through." Sermon topic and gift idea all in the same instant.

He grabbed the church keys and strode toward the door. He had to do some business with a carpenter—other that the One he'd just been talking to.

❄

"I can do this." Hoover caressed one of the maple planks leaning against the wall in the cluttered store room. "What's it from?"

"My old desk. It was actually a small conference table. When we decided to hire a secretary, we converted my office into two and the desk had to go. Dante dismantled it, but it was too nice to get rid of. Figured we'd find something to do with it."

"And now you have. I'll make it pretty."

"It's really short notice."

Hoover laughed. "I work best under pressure."

"You're sure it won't interfere with the new job?"

"I'm sure. That's only part-time."

"Okay. Good." Jay stretched his neck from one side to the other.

"You seem a bit stressed, Pastor Jay." Esther strutted at their feet, bobbing her head. She always seemed to be seconding Hoover's words. "Everything all right?"

The guy had honest eyes. The kind of person you could trust with secrets. At least he had that aura about him. Jay looked down at the chicken searching out stray bits of old popcorn and dehydrated box elder bugs on the basement floor. Could a person trust a person with a pet chicken? Something in his gut said yes. "Can I treat you to a cup of coffee, Hoover?"

"I'd like that. Many a problem has been solved over a good cup of joe."

"So true. There's a little shop about a block from here."

On the way to Mugs 'n Beans, Jay tried some gentle probing. "So, out of a job, huh?

"What?" Hoover appeared genuinely perplexed.

"Just wondering what brought you to us."

"Oh. That would be my boss."

Jay squinted at him. "What are you, an undercover cop?"

Hoover laughed. "Nah. My boss is the same as yours."

Funny. When Jay opened the coffee shop door, Hoover tapped Esther's head twice and she ducked into his coat. That had to be breaking some health code. There must be a No Pet Chickens Allowed ordinance still in effect from the 1800s.

Destiny, one of the girls Bethany mentored, stood behind the counter. "Hey, Pastor Jay. How about a gingerbread latte?"

"Might I suggest chamomile tea?" Hoover's eyes twinkled.

"Thank you for the tip. Maybe I'll take you up on it after Sunday." He ordered a large black coffee.

Hoover asked for green tea with honey. Jay shook his head. The guy didn't look like a health nut. "You remind me of one of my foster moms. She was one of those granola types." Why had he said that? He never talked about that part of his life.

"The way I figure it, this body's just on loan and I better take care of it the best I can."

"Point taken. I am sufficiently convicted. I'll skip the sugar. How's that for a start?"

Hoover thanked Destiny with a tip of his billed stocking cap. "Sugar is a tool of the devil, so I'd say that's a good starting place."

The only open table was in front of the counter. Jay took a chair with his back to the dessert case. "See no evil," he joked as he sat.

"So tell me about the Enterprise. Love the name, by the way. It's not like any shelter I've ever seen."

"It's not a shelter." Jay leaned back as he stirred his coffee. "About five years ago we had a congregational meeting to talk about impacting the community. We'd just opened Serenity with the idea that women could stay there up to six months after giving birth. At the meeting, one of the new moms mentioned she'd always wanted to own a gift shop, but how was a person supposed to start without money or a place to live? That was the spark. The church was only using a couple of the classrooms in the school. The thing was run down—way more than what you see. So we went in search of backers." He told him about the various residents and the nine businesses they'd started so far. "Sandy over there started this coffee shop with her husband. He passed away last year. You can imagine how good it is for her to have all this support."

Hoover looked around and nodded.

"Two of the businesses failed, but that's not bad for this part of town."

"Not bad at all." Hoover bounced his tea bag. "So why did you let me in?"

"We're not a shelter, but we have one apartment we make available for people in need. Not that you're in need." Though he didn't know the first thing about the guy. "We've housed a few missionaries too."

"Well, I guess I could come under that category."

Something bumped the back of his chair and Jay turned to see Destiny easing a seven-layer chocolate cake out of the pie case. "Yum."

"But we must guard our eyes." Hoover wrapped the string of his teabag around his spoon and squeezed it. "Which brings me to a question. You and Bethany?"

"That's not a question." Way to stall. He needed a second to figure out where to start.

"I think it is a question in your mind. How long have you known her?"

"I first met her seven years ago. She grew up in Holly Park and she'd come back to visit her dad fairly often, but we'd never had anything other than a hi-how-are-you conversation until five months ago when she and her daughter moved back. Did you know she has a nine-year-old daughter?"

"That complicates things?"

"Not really. I love that kid." He looked across the room. Outside, streetlights flickered on, then off, finally deciding the sun was done working for the day and it was their turn. He filled his lungs and let out a long, slow breath. "What complicates things is that Bethany Schmidt is pregnant."

"Oh, Pastor. I'm so sorry." Hoover lowered his voice as he leaned in and held a finger to his mouth. He nodded toward a spot to Jay's right. Destiny stood wiping down the counter with meticulous care. Eavesdropping. She couldn't have heard anything, could she?

Hoover put a hand on his shoulder "Poor Bethany. Not unlike the Christmas story you're acting out, is it?"

"The similarities are eerier than you know."

"What does this mean for you? Will you be asked to resign?"

"No." He rubbed his eyes with a hand warm from hugging his cup. "The baby's not mine. I won't suffer a thing unless . . ."

Hoover nodded. The pressure of his hand tightened. "Unless you decide to do the Joseph thing."

"Yes."

"Does she want you to?"

"I have no idea. I've only known about it since Friday and every time we get close to talking about it, something or someone interrupts."

"May I give you some advice?"

"Of course."

"If you really feel this is what God is asking you to do, don't let anyone or anything get in your way. Especially yourself."

Jay nodded, once again feeling a Joseph kind of conviction. "I won't." He squared his shoulders. "I'll talk to her tomorrow. First thing. Or second." He grinned and shrugged his shoulders.

The blue of Hoover's eyes seemed to deepen. His finger swiped the air in the same kind of gesture Dante used in his angel proclamations from the orange crate. "Do not be afraid, Pastor Jay."

Chapter Eight

The women of Bethlehem Community met on Monday to throw a Christmas party for the women and children of Serenity. But first, they gathered in the church kitchen to wrap gifts and devour lunch. When the chip bowls emptied and the towers of sandwiches dwindled to crumbs, Bethany led the procession of eleven women laden with wrapped packages, baskets of fruit, and boxes of cookies.

Misty opened the door. *"Feliz Navidad!"* Her hair was green today, with one bright red stripe hanging over her left cheek. From the cell phone in her pocket, Pentatonix crooned "That's Christmas to Me." The house smelled of cloves and cinnamon and whispered of hope. In the three months since Misty had gone from volunteer to fulltime housemother, she'd transformed the place, both in décor and emotional atmosphere.

"Hi." A tiny head of dark curls peeked from behind Misty's leg. Bethany handed three stacked trays of cookies to Misty and scooped him up. "How are you, Jerome? Excited for Christmas?"

The curls jiggled as he nodded. "Did you bring prethenths?"

"Hmm . . . Isn't that Santa's job?"

"He's not real. Wanna see my thtocking?"

"Absolutely." She followed him to the "fireplace" Misty had painted between the two front windows. Seven stockings, crocheted by women from the church, hung from nails. The last one was smaller than Bethany's hand—in hopes Jerome's little sister would be born before Christmas. *Five days left, little one.*

"Look, it haths my name . . . on . . . ith wet! Mom! My thtocking ith all wet!"

Hands on the small of her back to counterbalance the weight of a belly that couldn't stretch much bigger, Jocelyn Charles swayed into the room. "Misty! We need buckets again."

In seconds, Misty appeared with a stack of towels and Cool Whip containers. She looked at Bethany and shrugged one shoulder. "All I want for Chrithmuth ith a roof without leakths."

"Next year."

"Really? You know something I don't?"

"I know that my dad's answer for everything budget-related is 'next year.'"

Misty laughed and ushered two pregnant women, one mom with a five-month-old on her hip, and Jerome to the dining room where the church ladies had set out a spread of goodies. While Misty prayed, Bethany squeezed Jerome's stocking in a faded towel, praying the reds and greens wouldn't bleed into the white letters of his name. She stared at a rust-tinged rivulet—snow melting through nail holes in a poorly insulated flat roof. This part of the house had once been a screened porch. Where did this fix-up project land on a too-long repair list?

As she watched water trickle down the newly painted fireplace and drip into a plastic container on the window sill, she thought of yesterday's sermon. *Is God calling us this week to say yes to something we can't accomplish in our own strength? Is He asking us—each of us individually and Bethlehem Community as a whole—to trust Him to lead us out of what is familiar and comfortable?*

If she took the job in St. Louis, she could set money aside for repairs on Serenity.

Jerome toddled over on chubby legs, cookie in one hand, candy cane in the other. "Ith my thtocking dry?" Golden brown eyes looked at her with trust and expectation.

She opened the towel. White letters were still white. As she breathed a sigh, Jerome hugged her arm, smashing sugar cookie into her favorite ugly Christmas sweater. "I love you, Bethany. You're my hero."

There were other ways to make money. In a town with this little boy and a man who just might be in love with her. "I love you too, sweetie." She kissed the soft curls. *And I'm staying right here.*

❄

Jay seemed distracted on Tuesday, which was fine with Bethany. She'd made plans to meet her dad for lunch, so she had a quick answer when Jay asked if she wanted to order subs. The rest of the day they'd each stayed in their own ten-by-ten offices and their only contact had been short messages—"Laverne on line one for you." "What's the date of the ladies' retreat?" Nothing personal.

Now it was four o'clock and she breathed a sigh of relief. Rehearsal started at six and she could hear a buzz of people gathering to set up props and lighting. The pizza she'd ordered for cast and crew would arrive at five, but she was ducking out for a quick supper with Sarah before that and going out for coffee with Misty after rehearsal. No gaps in her evening—no chance for being alone with Jay tonight. Or the rest of the week. He'd be out of the office for a pastors' meeting tomorrow and months ago she'd asked off for Thursday and Friday to spend it with Ava.

She'd made it. Sometime after Sunday she'd tell him they had to talk. For now, she was home free. She slipped into her jacket, zipped it, and grabbed her purse and gloves.

And her office door opened. And closed behind Jay.

"Hi. What's up?" Her voice was light and airy. Her insides felt like solidifying lava. Jay wasn't smiling.

"Bethany, we need to talk."

Her knees bent reflexively and she sat in her desk chair. He took a folding chair from next to her bookshelf and set it close enough that she was sure their knees would touch. "We need to talk about that call I got on Friday at your place."

"Call?"

"From 'Dr. M's' office."

"Dr. M? I don't know any—" Chunks of hardened volcanic material rose to her esophagus. The job. Dr. Morganstein. "Oh, Jay. I'm so sorry. I was just waiting for the right time to talk to you about it."

He sat. An inch separated them. But the look on his face made it seem less.

"I was kind of a mess after I moved back, still recovering from the breakup and I was restless. I wasn't sure this was where I wanted to stay. So I started looking around. But things are different now. Our relationship changes everything. I know I'm assuming a lot, but it feels like something's happening between us and, unless I'm wrong about your feelings, I'm not going to keep it."

His eyes froze her.

"Jay? What are you thinking?"

"That I can't believe what I just heard."

"Can't believe in a good way? I thought you'd be happy."

He squinted as if he had a headache. "Bethany. This is ridiculous. I'm sure you're scared but have you considered that this might be your last chance for this? And have you thought about what's best for Ava?"

You want me to leave? She tried to say it, but her throat was too tight. She blinked away tears.

He stood, put his hand on her shoulder, and said, "Take your time. Pray about it."

"I already have." *And I chose you.*

"Then . . . " Jay stared at her for an eternal moment then turned and walked out.

❄

"Men." Bethany shoved a forkful of chef salad into her mouth. "How do you do it?"

Her sister laughed. "I give him a pass. And then I give him another one."

"He sounded like he wanted me to leave, but I know him. He's mad and he's being passive aggressive."

"Maybe he genuinely wants you to be happy. He doesn't want to stand in the way of what's best for you."

"But I want him to want me. Why can't he just ask me to stay?"

"Because he's a man." Sarah took a bite of sandwich. "Sexist, I know," she said with her mouth full. "But true for him."

"I want to stay here so you can watch my belly grow and feel the babies kick."

"Ba*by*."

They had all agreed on a single egg transfer. The idea of implanting several embryos with the intention of terminating one or more was absolutely not an option. Sarah had changed doctors early in the process because the first one felt it imperative to start with multiple embryos. "More chance of success, more cost effective," he'd said. "Not a chance," Dave had answered, ushering his wife and sister-in-law out the door. But she'd read about studies that showed an increase in the chance of an embryo "twinning" in IVF.

"Just preparing my brain. And yours."

"So . . . Jay is—"

75

"Let's stick with baby. Or babies. I made an appointment for my first injection on the second of January."

"What time? I'll come with you."

"Seven-thirty."

"My treat for breakfast after."

"Deal. My treat for your first appointment. You and Dave should plan a fertilization party."

Sarah curled her lip. "So romantic. Which brings us back to Pastor Jay."

Bethany glanced at the time on her phone. "The good news is he's so ticked about the job I may never have to tell him about the surrogacy."

With a sigh, Sarah pushed her plate aside. "That boy loves you."

"You can't know that."

"No." Sarah stared over Bethany's shoulder, eyes glimmering. "But Dad can."

"What did he say?"

"I'm not supposed to tell you."

"But you will." Bethany patted her belly. "Because I have leverage."

Sarah's gaze swept the ceiling. "This is going to be a very long year."

"Spill."

"Jay showed up at Dad's Saturday night while we were still there and asked to talk privately."

"And?"

"And you'll just have to wait and see."

❄

Jay's running shoes slapped hard-packed snow, footfalls echoing off the corrugated metal side of an abandoned warehouse. It wasn't a safe place to run at this time of day with the sun creeping low on the horizon, but he had to do something with the shock-induced adrenaline electrifying his nerves. Had to find some semblance of calm before rehearsal.

His breath crystalized in white puffs of frustration. Three days ago Bethany had kissed him with such tenderness and passion he'd thought the wires in his brain would fuse in one solid mass of incredible. In that moment he'd felt like everything he ever longed for had been met in Bethany Schmidt. She was his present and his future and years of abandonment, rejection, and self-doubt vanished in her arms. They were likeminded, meant for each other, one in every way except physical. He could have proposed right there in front of the Green Goose and never looked back. It didn't matter that she had a child by one man and was pregnant by another. He was ready to take on the world and Bethany and Ava and a baby.

That kiss had given him the courage to talk to Bernard. He hadn't stuttered or fumbled when he told the man he loved his daughter and wanted his blessing to begin courting her with the intention of marrying her in the near future.

He'd expected a bear hug and a thank you-for-covering-my-daughter's-shame speech. Not hesitation.

Bernard had glanced back toward the living room where Sarah and David sat holding hands and whispering. "You're willing to wait a year?" he'd asked. "Or more?"

"Why?" Under the circumstances, wouldn't he want her married as soon as possible?

"I want my girl to have a proper wedding with the dress of her dreams and she'll need time to get back to the size she wants to be."

Ah. "Of course." He could wait a year. Joseph did. Though he took Mary to be his wife, they were just roommates until after Jesus was born.

"You think you've got what it takes to put up with everything she'll be going through? Mood swings and cravings and all that?"

77

Bernard had laughed. Jay was shocked at the almost giddy tone of his voice. Bernard Schmidt was a pillar of the church, a man who wasn't afraid to talk of his mistakes, but who held himself and the other elders to high moral standards. Jay was disappointed to see the rules didn't seem to apply to his daughter. Not that he'd want to hear him putting her down, but this attitude seemed to completely discount her sin.

"I'm willing, and I believe God will give me the strength to be there for her."

Then the bear hug came. "You have my blessing, son. I would be honored."

But that was yesterday.

What would Bernard do when he discovered his daughter's intentions?

❄

"Don't be scared, Mary. God really likes you." Dante, towering over Bethany on the crate that was now covered in glitter-dusted cotton batting, pointed like a principal disciplining a truant child.

Though she'd dragged herself into rehearsal by sheer force, the intensity of his words made her want to laugh. Yolanda stood in the aisle, hands planted on hips covered in blue satin. She'd found an old choir robe in the attic and decided it was the appropriate director attire. The look on her face said, "Don't you dare." Bethany pressed her lips together.

"You're going to be pregnant and that baby's a boy."

The angel choir tittered. Out of the corner of her eye, Bethany watched three of her teen girls—Lena, Mackenzie, and Destiny—whispering behind white-gloved hands. She turned her head just enough to allow her to stare at the girls around Dante's right elbow. Mackenzie glared at Lena and Destiny.

You're going to be pregnant . . . Bethany camped on those words while Dante paused for dramatic effect. *I'm going to be pregnant*. Seven or eight months from now, she could be feeling kicks and rolls and hiccups.

". . . give him the name Jesus. He's going to be awesome—more awesome than any awesome you've ever seen—and they'll call him the son of the Most High God . . ."

If the girls were laughing now, how would they react when she really was pregnant? She and Dave and Sarah had talked about what and when to tell people. Sarah wanted to avoid prying and gossip. Bethany was on board with that. She could just imagine the saccharine smiles of some of the church ladies. *So, dear, did it take?* But if she didn't tell people about the IVF ahead of time, they'd think she was making it up.

Dante cleared his throat. "How can . . ."

She didn't need to fake the look of bewilderment. "How can that happen? I'm still a virgin!"

The angel choir fell apart. Destiny snorted. Lena doubled over. In a nano second, twelve girls were LOL in a most unangel-like way. All but one. MacKenzie stood to the side, arms folded, chin jutted out.

"Cut!"

Chapter Nine

"*H*ey Joseph, don't freak out about asking Mary to marry you because that baby's real daddy . . ."

Is *who*? Jay was determined to deadpan his way through rehearsal. Show no emotion. Feel no emotion. It wasn't working. The run had done nothing but make him sweaty. And then chilled to the core. The hot shower had made him late. When he got to the sanctuary, the entire cast was assembled around Yolanda and she was doing his job. Praying. "Lord, Jesus, puh*lease* let us get through this without stopping for any reason. Puh*lease* protect us from forgotten lines and flat notes and falling props."

"And falling pastors," Dante had added, cracking up the group until Yolanda stomped a high-heeled boot and silence reigned once more.

Focus. Listen to Dante. Remember your lines. Forget Bethany. Forget what she's going to do. Forget she didn't have the decency to tell you herself. Forget that Ava will be heartbroken. Forget that her father—

"Jay?" Dante whispered. "You're gonna call him Jesus!"

Yolanda sighed.

Jay jumped up, took two strides across the old red carpeting to where Bethany stood, looking angelic and pure and innocent. And honest.

What was Joseph really thinking at this point? He could imagine the thoughts: *Sure. "Don't be afraid,'" he says. Am I really supposed to just shut up and let people think the worst? I've been a God-fearing, law-following guy all my life. No black marks on my permanent record. Not a one. Never been stopped for racing a donkey through town or partying too hardy with the Passover wine. Never looked twice at another man's wife. Blocked every one of those thoughts about what's behind those veils. I'm a good guy. Everyone respects me. And now this? A woman brings me down? I could run. Or lie. But if this is really what God wants me to do . . .*

Jay put his arm around Bethany.

And the angel choir cheered.

"Cut!"

❄

"You and I are only human." Jay sang the words and fought the feelings. They held hands across an empty manger. He didn't know where to look. This was the point where Yolanda, in an early practice, had burst out singing, "The look of love is in your eyes . . ." He turned away from Bethany's face, but every time he bowed his head, he saw the protruding belly. Wouldn't be long before she could play the part without the pillow. Too bad she hadn't gotten pregnant a few months earlier, she could have— *Stop!* Sarcasm was nothing but ugly. He forced himself to look her in the eye.

She gave a sad, weak smile and began to sing. "We can't do this on our own."

"But you and I are not alone." He sang the answer. Bethany and the choir joined in on the refrain. "God will guide us, help us, change us. God will change us, you and I."

Bethany's eyes filled with tears. Jay's heart squeezed. Anger dripped out of it until it was wrung dry. *How is it possible I still love her?* They kneeled and their half of the stage went black as the spotlight lit the shepherds. Bethany closed her eyes. He knew that look. Did she know her lips moved ever so slightly when she prayed? He closed his eyes and did the same. *I can't help it, Lord, I love this woman. I could have loved this child. But she's not going to give me the chance.*

❄

Bethany willed the tears pressing against the back of her eyes not to fall. Kneeling beside the manger, she looked out at their audience of one ponytailed man with a chicken on his lap. Hoover would think she was over-playing the part. In the dark, she tugged the pillow out from under her robe and slid it behind a hay bale. Jay pulled the cloth-wrapped doll from behind the other side of the bale. Five minutes in the dark with Jay felt like an eternity.

The angel choir had recovered from their giggle fit and sang with angelic clarity. "Hark, you shepherds, wake up and sing. Jesus is born. Come worship the King!" They stepped side to side with the gospel beat. MacKenzie, with her copper curls. Lena, pale, blond, covered with tattoos, and Destiny, whose mother was Puerto Rican and father was African American. All thirteen girls, street smart and toughened by life, hurting in so many ways, but trying. "Stand up now shepherds, follow the light. Come see a miracle, born on this night."

❄

Bethany rocked the swaddled doll as the spotlight slowly widened on the stable and Yolanda's rich soprano filled the room. "Silent Night. Holy Night. All is calm. All is bright."

Mary, what was it like for you? Was Joseph supportive? Did he breathe with you through contractions and tell you he loved you and he'd always be there for you? Did he rub your back and hold your hand and sing to you? Did he pray over you and your baby? Or did he leave you alone? Did you go through labor alone, or attended by strangers when you only wanted one person by your side?

Bethany gazed down, remembering the first time she held Ava. Sarah, Misty, and Rick's mother had been in and out, taking turns coaching her through fourteen hours of labor, but she'd asked for time alone with her daughter before Ava's grandfathers met her. As she'd studied the curve of her ears, the heart shape of her mouth, she'd felt connected with every woman who'd ever given birth. She was a mother, a woman with purpose. As the sun rose, casting pink light across the bed, the sadness that had weighed her down for the past seven months transformed into determination. Everything her father had told her about God suddenly rang true. How could there not be a God? This tiny perfection was not a product of chance. And if there was a God, He had a plan for both of them.

Determination had filled her soul in that newborn moment and a similar feeling swept over her again. Self-pity would not win here. Ava would be home in two days and she would not allow Jay Davidson and his unforgiving pride to tarnish her Christmas.

On the other side of the stage, sheep made from old fleece-lined coats collected from Goodwill nestled beside a rag-tag band of shepherds. Starlight from the disco ball above the stable sprinkled the carpet, spilled over the angel choir, and dotted Misty's red and green hair as she stood ready to read the closing words.

Why had she ever wanted to leave? What would she find in St. Louis to replace this? No career, no income or success, could take the place of this family. But now, if Jay couldn't get beyond— She froze the thought. Negativity not allowed. She knew how to do Christmas without a man. She breathed in the scent of myrrh from the diffuser behind the Christmas tree and closed her eyes and rocked just as Mary must have done.

"Son of God, love's pure light. Radiant beams from Thy holy fa—"

Bawk! Esther hopped onto the back of a cardboard donkey. A shepherd gasped. The donkey wobbled. Yolanda yelled into her mic, "Get that bird off my stage!" Esther startled, squawked, and flapped. The motion set the donkey rocking. "Don't you *even!*" A collectively held breath—in which Bethany imagined the domino effect of bawking chicken, tipping donkey, fleeing shepherds, rolling sheep, hysterical angels—slowly released as the wobbling slowed and stopped and Esther hopped daintily onto the top of the piano.

Shepherds high-fived, angels quietly cheered, Esther strutted atop the old Whitney spinet, and Yolanda said, "That, people, is why we pray."

Bethany smiled down at the babe in her arms and whispered, "All is calm."

And she would do everything in her power to keep it that way.

❊

Jay tossed the bathrobe on the front pew as Bethany and Misty walked down the aisle toward the back of the church followed by MacKenzie, who shot him a parting look that singed his eyebrows. What was that all about?

Yolanda snatched the robe and folded it. "Those girls left in a hurry."

"They had plans."

"Seems to me one of 'em was runnin' away from sumpin'. What you think, Hoover? You see the way Miss Bethany flew outa here without helping clean up? Something's up."

Hoover looked up from the donkey he'd laid on its side. "I think I'm going to remake this thing out of plywood and give it a proper stand, that's what I think."

"Come on. You seem pretty astute. Got any advice for the lovelorn over here?"

"Already gave him advice. Told him to ask God and do what he's told."

"Can't argue with that. Never will. But God don't always send a script. We need to come up with some words for this boy." She lowered herself onto the edge of the platform, landed with a thud, and arranged folds of blue satin to cover knees held apart by the ampleness of her thighs.

Knowing it would do him no good to attempt an exit, Jay sat and faced her, waiting for his "script."

"You being gentle with that girl, Pastor Jay? You being patient? She's got feelings for you, for sure, but we all know why she came back here, right? That girl was hurting something fierce and it ain't easy to start trusting again. You gotta woo her slow."

Jay sighed. If wooing Bethany "slow" was his biggest problem right now, he'd be one happy man. He rubbed his face. "Things aren't always the way they seem, Yolanda. Right now I need some Solomon wisdom and some—"

The walls reverberated with the clang of the massive front door slamming. Footsteps echoed off the walls of the narthex. MacKenzie, wearing skinny jeans, a too-thin jacket, and a black and white scarf coiled around her neck like a boa constrictor, marched toward them. Angel glitter clung to her hair but there was nothing angelic about the rage that contorted her face.

"MacKenzie, what's—?"

"I was gonna keep out of this. It's none of my business. But Bethany's like the sister I always wanted or the mama I never had or maybe both all rolled into one, so I gotta say this. I saw her leave without talking to you and I don't know what's happening, but you better not hurt her or you'll have every kid in this church in your face and we're gonna tell our parents and they're gonna get you fired. You can't go playing Joseph if you can't do it in real life. You better marry her and give that baby a home and a daddy, you hear?"

Yolanda's mouth flopped open, but, for the first time since he'd met her, nothing came out.

❄

Misty hugged a steaming mug. "Give him time."

"Maybe a clean break would be easier."

"You've made a couple of those." Misty arched one brow.

"Ouch. Wow. What is it the Bible says about the wounds of a friend?"

"They can be trusted."

"But they hurt." Especially when they were accurate. She'd run home to daddy after Rick died and again after Peter dumped her.

"I'm kidding." Misty shook her head. "You used to know when I was joking. You seriously made the right call when you came back. Both times. You will this time. Selfishly, I hope the right call is 'Stay' because I like having you around."

Sandy caught Bethany's eye and lifted a hot water pot. "Need more?"

Bethany nodded and set her cup down.

As she poured, Sandy said, "Peppermint's good for the tummy, isn't it?"

"I've heard that."

"I keep a stash of Saltines behind the counter for the Serenity girls. My grandma gave me peppermint tea and soda crackers when I was pregnant. Got me through the day."

Misty nodded. "You take good care of our moms, Sandy."

"I was there once myself." She patted Bethany's shoulder. "Pregnant at Christmas, too. I know what it's like." She waved with her fingertips as she walked back to the counter.

"She's in an odd mood." Bethany pressed pie crumbs with her fork. "Everybody's in an odd mood."

"It's just Christmas. Speaking of, what can I do for Sunday?"

"You can wave a magic wand and make the church basement look cozy and Christmasy. All of the decorations look old." She rested her chin in her hand. "Sorry I'm in such a crummy mood. How do I get out of this before Ava gets home? She's had a week of sledding and making ornaments and sleeping in a room with her own Christmas tree. I have to make this special, but I just feel . . ." She was sure there was a word to end the sentence, but it wasn't coming to mind.

"You just feel sad and in love."

Bethany blew out a breath that caused her napkin to flutter onto Misty's plate. "How does a person know when it's worth fighting for? Should I go pound on his door and tell him he's making way too much out of this and if he really has feelings for me he should take me in his arms and kiss me and tell me not to go to St. Louis? Or do I just give up on him and start over in a new town?"

"Remember the 'what ifs' we started on Friday?"

Bethany nodded.

"What if you move? Will you always be wishing you'd tried harder with Jay or will you feel like you saved yourself from heartache?"

"I . . ." Another sentence without an end. She stared out the front window. A middle-aged couple strolled through a halo of lamplight holding hands followed by an old man walking his dog. The couple laughed. The man shuffled as if the dog were his only friend in the world and they had no one waiting for them at home.

Across the street, colored lights outlined the front window of a house she'd helped paint in August, just before the husband came home from his deployment. A lit tree glowed from behind the window. This would be a happy Christmas. "I want to belong to someone."

Chapter Ten

*A*fter closing on Tuesday night, Elizabeth stood in the work room of the store, searching for a light bulb for her desk lamp. The room was a mess. She hated disorganization, but this was Nora's territory. The door opened. *Speaking of disorder.* Nora set a mug on the cluttered work table. Coffee sloshed onto a roll of silver metallic ribbon. She ran a hand through her hair. Frizzed ends, two inches of gray roots. "I don't like the brown. Too depressing."

For a split second Elizabeth thought she was talking about the mess she'd just made. Or the reason for the lack of color in her hair. *I don't like it either.* "The tree? I think it's classy. Kelsey did a nice job." Blame it on hormones, but she was not feeling conciliatory tonight.

"Too Thanksgivingish."

"But with all those gold stars and—"

"Change it. I left that tree undecorated for a reason. Some people need blank canvases."

Elizabeth chewed on the tip of her tongue and stared at the jumble of tangled garland and rope lights spilling out of a bin behind Nora. What she wouldn't give to turn this room into a blank canvas—empty the shelves, clear the tables, and organize everything in well-marked stations. She'd arrange ribbon by the colors of the rainbow. Reds to purples. She'd put a shelf next to the printer with every hue and texture of paper known to woman. Scissors in one drawer. Tape in another. Everything at her fingertips.

But this wasn't her store. How would she handle this mess come summer when the "nesting instinct" her friends talked about turned her into more of a tidy-freak than she already was? Blame it on hormones, or not wanting to go home to an empty house three days before Christmas, but something gave her the courage to fake a smile and open her mouth. "How about if I do a little systematizing in here?"

Nora stopped rummaging through a mound of gold-edged leaves and glittered pinecones. Unplucked brows converged. "What for?"

Long, slow breath. Candle blow. Good Lamaze practice. By mid-summer, she'd be well trained for childbirth. "Well, I think we'd save time, which is money, if things were more"— *unhoarderlooking*—"categorized."

Nora pulled a tape measure from under the gilded-forest pile with a look of triumph. She picked up her coffee cup. Another slosh on silver ribbon. "Don't you have a life, Elizabeth? Go home to your husband. Watch *White Christmas*. Drink egg nog." She opened the door, slopped coffee on her rumpled pink shirt, and let the door slam behind her.

And Elizabeth burst into tears.

❄

Don't you have a life, Elizabeth? The words had a life, jeering at her like a living, breathing specter, taunting her moments of near sleep. At three a.m., she threw a pillow at the clock, got up, and walked out to the living room. She flipped a switch, waking the fiber optic trees. Blue and white. Boring. Decorated by a person with no passion or purpose or plan. The same kind of person who thought browns were festive.

No wonder James didn't get into Christmas. She'd always made it chic and sophisticated, not whimsical and nostalgic. She padded back to the bedroom and put on her slippers and robe. Somewhere in the basement, in a labeled box in the holiday section, were the ornaments James's mother had given him each year as he was growing up. In another, she'd find the ones she'd made with her grandmother throughout her childhood. This year, they'd start a new tradition. Christmas with meaning.

The boxes were on a top shelf. She found the stepstool and reached them easily. Not too heavy. She stacked them and headed for the stairs then stopped. The pale yellow storage container was almost hidden by a sheet of drywall leaning against the shelf. Why hadn't she donated that stuff long ago? Why hadn't James snuck it out of the house and taken it to Goodwill when she wasn't looking? She set the boxes down, moved the stepstool, and lowered the bin.

Baby clothes. Bought at a going-out-of-business sale the second year they were married. Such a good deal and they had so little money. *Why not stock up now?* Because getting pregnant was a given, wasn't it? She closed her eyes before lifting the lid. *Please, no moth holes or mildew or mouse droppings.*

Perfect. Everything inside was as pristine as the hopeful day she'd bought a gender-neutral bin to store it in. Onesies, sleepers, sweaters and receiving blankets in green, white, and yellow.

And at the bottom . . . a pair of tiny white shoes.

❄

A strange combination of grogginess and anticipation messed with Elizabeth's concentration on Wednesday afternoon. She walked around the Christmas tree display, clipboard in hand, trying to look official. But this was not store business. This was personal.

She was shopping.

When James walked in the house tomorrow night he'd be greeted by a tree that looked real. She'd take Nora's blank slate and cover it with memories and dreams. Nostalgia and whimsy. To the ornaments she'd found in the basement she'd add strings of glass beads that looked like popcorn and cranberries. She'd drape each branch in old-fashioned silver tinsel and circle the tree with big, vintage-looking colored lights. In James's box, she'd found a tree skirt quilted by his grandmother, a gift for their first Christmas. A stab of guilt. James's grandmother had passed away ten years ago. How could she have been so crass as to relegate a keepsake made by the woman's own hands to a shelf in the basement?

From now on, things would be different. All color. No more boring white. Except for the focal point of the tree. A tiny pair of baby shoes.

At five a.m. she had finished foraging in the basement and moved to the attic. There she'd found the perfect Christmas gift for James. Not that she hadn't already bought him half a dozen things—Packer tickets and new bicycle gloves and a box of emoji-faced golf balls. But this was the gift he'd remember. Forever.

In the far corner of an attic that hadn't been cleaned since they moved in seventeen years ago, sat a cradle. Handmade by James's dad before he was born. When they'd moved to a condo, her-father-in-law had brought it over, proudly setting it in the living room. "Might as well just sit here," he'd said, slapping James on the back. Another expectation James had failed to meet. She had no idea when he'd stuffed it in the attic.

The cradle needed a coat of paint. Red maybe. Something more festive than brown. Come summer, she could paint it pink or blue—one of the pops of color in the lemon chiffon room. For now, it needed to be old-fashioned-Christmasy.

"Kelsey?" She waved the girl over.

"Huh?"

"Can you keep an eye on things if I dash out for an hour?"

"Yep."

"Thanks." Strange that she felt confident leaving the store in the hands of this monosyllabic millennial. The girl had potential.

"Where ya' goin'?"

Buried potential. "I've got an idea for a display. I'm going to the paint store."

❄

Shannon waved from behind the half-circle counter as Elizabeth walked in. "Hey, my preggers friend! How are you feeling?"

"Not bad. How are—"

A man rose from behind one end of the counter. A tall man with a ponytail. He wore an apron that matched Shannon's. "Ma'am." His hand rose to his forehead as if he was doffing his hat. Did people still do that?

"Elizabeth, this is Hoover, my saving grace."

"Delighted to meet you, Elizabeth."

"You too." What was it about the burly guy that made her want to add, "sir"? "Nice to meet Shannon's saving grace."

"Oh, I'm not worthy of that title, ladies. Goodness, what would Christmas be if *I* were the reason for the season?" He laughed at his own joke. "Are you here to visit with Shannon, or can I help you, Elizabeth?"

"Both, actually. I need some Christmasy red paint. I found an old cradle in the attic and I want to surprise my husband with it."

"A cradle, huh?" The man raised a brow but didn't wait for an explanation. "Let me bring you some samples." The ponytail bounced on his back as he walked away with giant strides.

"Seems like a nice guy. How's he working out?"

"Like a dream. I'm adopting him as my kid's grandpa. Isn't he sweet?"

"That means he'll be my kid's grandpa-in-law. That works."

"How are you feeling?"

"Amazingly good today considering I only got a couple hours of sleep."

"So you were out partying last night, huh?" Shannon winked.

"Partying in my basement." She described her revelation about the lack of color and tradition in her Christmas décor. "It just hit me that we're missing the real meaning of Christmas."

"Which is?" The ponytailed man appeared out of nowhere and handed her a fan of paint chips. "I'm thinking 'Rudolph Red.'"

She compared the one he pointed to with the others. "You're right. It has to be Rudolph. It's more Door County cherry red than tomato red." She winked at Shannon. "Another yummy color. And I'll paint it in the garage with the door open."

"Elizabeth is preg . . . oops." Shannon's lips stretched, exposing gritting teeth. "I'm sorry. I shouldn't have said—"

"It's okay." She turned to the man with the vacuum cleaner name. "I'm due the middle of summer. Still trying to get used to the idea. It was quite a surprise."

"Congratulations. You are both blessed. Children are a gift. Do you know what Psalm 139 says?" He looked from Elizabeth to Shannon. Apparently her child's future mother-in-law was as Bible illiterate as she was. "It says, 'For you created my inmost being; you knit me together in my mother's womb. I praise you because I am fearfully and wonderfully made; your works are wonderful, I know that full well. My frame was not hidden from you when I was made in the secret place, when I was woven together in the depths of the earth. Your eyes saw my unformed body; all the days ordained for me were written in your book before one of them came to be.'"

"Hmm." Shannon's mouth pursed. "I like that. This guy is like a walking Bible."

Elizabeth's thoughts were back at "knit together in my mother's womb." "Where is that again?" She had a Bible. Somewhere.

"I'll write it down for you." Hoover scribbled on a piece of paper and handed it to her. "And, since you were on the subject of the real meaning of Christmas, I'll give you this too." He handed her a flyer. "My church is putting on a program Friday night. I think you'd like it."

"I might go." Shannon pointed at the address. "Bethlehem Church is only a few blocks from here. Wanna go with me?"

"I don't know. My husband will be home." She couldn't imagine James wanting to spend Friday night in church. "But I'd like to."

Strange. She hadn't gone to church since middle school. But there was something compelling about the invite from this man with the honey-rich voice. She smiled at Hoover and pointed at the Rudolph chip. "I'd like a quart of this in satin."

❄

"I'm sorry, Kelsey. I thought it was stunning." Elizabeth tucked a plastic box under her arm and began lifting gold stars off the balsam.

"Anybody who's going to buy a ten-foot tree has already bought it. This thing isn't going to sell until next week. Why not make it look . . ."

Elizabeth's new phone ring—"Joy to the World"—accompanied Kelsey's tirade.

James. Calling at four in the afternoon? That would be three, mountain time. James never called her at work. What was wrong? She excused herself and strode toward her office as she answered. "James?"

"Hey!" he shouted. A roaring sound muffled his words.

"What's wrong?"

". . . at 11,900 feet. Thought I'd try to . . . windy up here. How are . . . feeling . . . and . . . hear me?"

"Kind of. That wind is really loud. I'm feeling good. I bought paint for our nursery."

"Can't wait either."

"For what?"

"Our anniversary."

Elizabeth sighed. "Having fun?"

"Gotta run too. Have to dress . . . Cocktails at five, you know."

No, I don't. The last time she'd dressed up and had a glass of anything that needed to be served in a stemmed glass was on their anniversary trip in February.

". . . tell you something. I'll try . . . airport tomorrow. Bye."

❄

Midnight. Elizabeth punched her pillow then tossed it across the room. Bunching the covers into a ball, she rolled on her side. This wasn't the way it was supposed to be. They'd wanted a baby for so long and then given up. Now here they were realizing an impossible dream, but nothing about it felt right.

Around one, she scooped her pillow off the floor and fell into a restless sleep. At 5:58 she woke in tears. Only a sliver of the dream that had caused them remained. One small, terrifying fact: In a few minutes, when James called from the airport, it would be to say good-bye. He wasn't coming home. At forty-three, the disruption of a child was more than he could handle.

The clock changed from 5:59 to 6:00 and her phone buzzed. She picked it up, took a ragged breath, and answered. James said "Hi" and she braced herself for what was coming. She would always remember this time. This moment her world stopped spinning. She was going to be a single mom. She was going to raise this chi—

Becky Melby

"I miss you."

"What?"

"Nobody should travel alone the week before Christmas. This place is full of families. It's got me reflecting."

Reflecting? James was reflecting? "About?"

"For one thing, about you quitting work after the first of the year. I hate that you're putting in so many hours. Especially now. What do you think?"

"I"—she didn't know she was crying until she tried to talk—"think you are wonderful."

"I love you. And I'll see you tonight. Okay if I make reservations at Carnevor?"

"Of course." Her answer came out weak, either from shock or the wave of wooziness brought on by the all-things-meat name. "Sounds wonderful."

"You're sure? Do you feel on top of things for Saturday? We can keep it really simple. Finger food maybe. And I'll do the shopping. I hate that Christmas is all on your shoulders this year."

This year? When had it ever been on his? Or theirs? "Thank you." If five days in Keystone did this, he could spend all of December in Colorado next year and she wouldn't utter a complaint. Except, she wouldn't be the only one with an opinion next year. She tucked her free arm close to her middle. *We'll keep him home, Joy.* "I talked to our moms at Thanksgiving. It's all figured out. They're bringing fondue and we're supplying all the stuff to dip."

"Perfect. You're the best planner. I'll do whatever you need when I get home."

"All I need is you." She wiped her face with her sleeve. How long had it been since she'd said those words? Or felt them? "Just come home."

"I will. I have something for you."

"What?"

"A surprise."

"Give me a hint."

"I bought it at a store I never thought I'd walk into."

A baby store. Or maternity. Or toy store? The tears flowed harder. "I love you."

"Bye, babes. See you soon."

Babes. He'd pluralized it. Tonight they'd be sitting together in front of a ten-foot balsam decorated with meaning. And little white shoes. "Bye."

Chapter Eleven

*A*va jumped out of her grandmother's car the second it stopped and charged toward Bethany as if she'd been gone five years instead of five days. "Mom! Look! Grandma got me a puppy!"

Bethany froze mid-laugh, looked down at the squirming brown fluff ball in Ava's arms then directed her gaze at the woman who should have become her mother-in-law. "Gloria?"

"Not to worry. He stays at our house. We named him Daughtry."

Daughtry. The name Rick gave to the mutt he found right before leaving for basic training. The dog that had kept his mom company in those long, dark first years after her only son died.

"He's adorable." Bethany hugged the wiggling, giggling armful of girl and dog and kissed the top of her daughter's head. In her mind she heard the words of "Home," Rick's favorite Daughtry song. She'd loved it when Rick sang it, but the words had turned bitter after he was gone and she was running home because she had no other option. Since Ava's birth, she'd seen the song as a prayer. *I'm coming home where I belong . . . I don't regret this life* You *chose for me . . .* Maybe she needed a new song. *I'm Staying Home Where I Belong.* Maybe.

"Can you come in for a bit?" Bethany asked, hoping Gloria would say no. Like that first day, nine years ago, she wanted time alone with Ava.

"Love to, but I can't."

"Okay." Not a surprise. She'd been here twice before and only once come into their apartment for a quick cup of tea. Bethany had a feeling being in the home she'd created for Ava just made it more real that Rick wasn't there. Gloria had to be thinking they'd probably be living in a lovely two story in a safe neighborhood near her if life had gone according to plan. To her credit, she'd never let her disapproval show, not even in the early years when Bethany was pulling the pieces of her exploded life together and Sam and Gloria would have had grounds for filing for custody.

"Everything still on for Sunday?"

"Yes." Now that was a surprise. She'd assumed it was just a polite offer and expected Sam and Gloria to back out of helping with the dinner. A two-hour drive to help people they didn't even know was out of character.

"Good. I'm heading to the store as soon as I get back to Wausau to get the cranberries. Two pounds enough?"

"That's what the notebook says they did last year. Seems like overkill to me. With the Enterprise and Serenity and"Grandma, can you stay long enough for me to show Pastor Jay my puppy?"

Bethany closed her eyes for the space of an inhale. "Oh, honey, Grandma has to get to the—"

"No worries. Of course you can show him. I'd like to meet this man I've been hearing about all week. Seems like he's right up there with"—she pointed at the stained glass window of Jesus kneeling in the garden—"Him."

Not at the moment, he isn't.

❋

99

Jay ran his hand along a sanded spindle. "Hoover, you do good work."

"Doesn't seem fitting to call a thing work when it brings so much pleasure." Hoover nudged Esther aside and reached for another piece of wood. "'Whatever your hand finds to do, do it all for the glory of God.' Love having busy hands." He began sanding again, then stopped. "How about you, Pastor Jay, are you loving what you do?"

"Most days. There are lots of times that don't feel like work. When I'm teaching, especially."

"Or singing to a beautiful woman? You've got quite the pipes."

Jay upended a five-gallon bucket and sat on it. "She's not keeping the baby."

"Oh, Pastor. Is she . . . ?"

"No. I don't think so. She said she's not keeping it. At least I assume she's talking adoption. I can't imagine Bethany . . . no."

"How's that hitting you?"

"Shock, I guess. She's such a good mom. Wait till you meet her daughter. I can't help wondering what this will do to her."

"Sounds like you'd found some peace about taking on two children who weren't yours."

Jay rubbed his chin. "I didn't realize I'd gotten so used to the idea. I guess what hurts is that she didn't even give me a chance. She says she made this decision *because* of me. Does she really think I'm the kind of guy who'd bail because she was pregnant?"

"But you're the kind of guy who'd bail when she talks about adoption."

"Wow. You don't pull any punches, do you?"

"Not my style."

"It's just so unlike her. I freaked."

"You felt left out of the decision."

Jay lowered his head to his hands. "She kissed me. Did I tell you that?"

"No, you didn't. And you think a kiss means you're privy to a say in all of her decisions?"

"Of course not." Then why had he stomped out? They'd had two dates. Sure, a lot of talks and walks and lunches had led up to those two dates, but they didn't have a commitment. "Okay. Maybe."

"You do realize she's got time to change her mind, right?"

"Well"—Jay gave a sheepish smile—"I suppose I should have realized that. She just sounded so sure."

"I'd say you've got quite a few months to show her— patiently, as Yolanda would say—that you're there for her. No matter what. That is if—"

"Pastor Jay! Where are you? I hafta show you something!"

As Ava's voice grew nearer, Jay shot Hoover a panicked look. The man calmly bent, picked up a tarp, and unfurled it over the wood.

The motion spooked Esther, who spurted out of the furnace room like she'd been shot from a cannon.

A dog yapped. Esther crowed. And Ava screamed.

The site that greeted Jay when he rushed into the fellowship hall was beyond ridiculous. Ava danced on tiptoes along the top of a banquet table, clutching a shaking, barking puppy while Esther hopped from chair to chair around the table, squawking what Jay could only translate as a greeting.

"She won't hurt you, Ava. Her name is Esther and I think she just wants to meet you and your friend."

Ava stopped prancing. "She's a pet?"

"Yep. Belongs to my friend Hoover here." He gestured toward Hoover then reached up for Ava and lowered girl and dog to the floor. "Welcome home. Who's this?"

"This is Daughtry, my dog."

"Your dog? Your mom is letting you—"

"The dog is staying with Ava's grandmother." Bethany crossed the room, followed by a woman with chemically red hair. "Pastor Jay, Hoover, this is Ava's grandmother, Gloria Bartlett." Nothing even remotely resembling a smile altered the expressionless set of Bethany's face.

Gloria extended her hand, first to Hoover, then to Jay. "Very nice to meet you. I've heard so much about the amazing Pastor Jay."

Jay took the dog from Ava's outstretched arms and nestled his face in gold fur. The warm smell of puppy stirred a long-slumbering wish. Every kid needed a dog. "Believe everything you hear if it makes me sound amazing." He glanced at Bethany. Maybe looks couldn't kill, but they sure did a lot of stabbing and slashing. He handed the dog back.

"Ava tells me all the kids love you."

Except for the one who won't get the chance. He smiled wider than he felt. "Might have something to do with these." He pulled a bag of WarHead candies from his pocket. Three adults made sour faces. Ava took two.

"I think it's more than—"

"Ava, we should let Grandma get on her way and I have everything set up for cut-out cookies."

Ava pouted. "Mom, can't we keep Daughtry? I promise I'll walk him and feed him and clean up his messes. He's practically house broken already. And he's my Christmas present. I can't spend Christmas without . . ."

As Ava presented her case, Jay laughed. And immediately felt the reproof from Bethany. Didn't she know every kid should have a dog? Didn't she know this begging and whining and *pleeease*-can-we-keep-him was a rite of passage? His childhood would have been so different if he'd had a pet to call his own.

Something that was actually his. His lips parted, but he forced back the words.

Hoover winked and gave the slightest nod.

"We could keep him in the office during the day and he could stay with me any time you're gone." The glimmer of hope in Ava's eyes spurred him on. "Or all the time." Jay was sure his pouty face matched the nine-year-old's. "Bethany?" Her name came out with too much emotion. Too much *pleeease.* Would she know he wasn't just talking about the dog?

Gloria cocked her head, joining the crowd of pleading faces. Of course she'd be on his side. Did she really want the hassle of housebreaking a puppy at her stage of life? No, that was a job suited to a full-time pastor who spent half of his time visiting parishioners in hospitals, prisons, and nursing homes. A full-time pastor the week before Christmas. *What were you thinking?*

"Fine. If Jay wants to keep him, it's fine with me." Bethany turned and walked out. She was anything but fine.

Ava dove at Jay. Her free arm wrapped around his waist. "You're the bestest best." She ran after Bethany, yelling over her shoulder, "I'll get his food and his bed and his dishes and I'll be right back."

Gloria extended her hand again. "Pastor Jay, I think I have to agree. You are the bestest best."

When the room became silent except for the drip of the kitchen sink and the scratching of a chicken under a table, Jay turned to Hoover. "What have I done?"

"I'm wondering that myself, Pastor." Hoover's eyes twinkled. "I'm thinking maybe an end around is at play here."

"Meaning?"

"You're using the girl to get to the mom."

"I'd nev . . . er." Was that what he was doing? Subconsciously? And if so, was he doing it to get back at her or win her over? *And they say women's brains are complicated.*

Hoover picked up the cordless drill. "Not that I'm saying that's a bad thing, mind you." Over the whine of the drill he said, "Time will tell, Pastor. Time will tell."

❋

Bethany took the bowl of chilled dough out of the refrigerator and clunked it onto the kitchen table. Across from her, Ava sorted cookie cutters. "Where's the bent Christmas tree? I want to make some of those for Jerome. Did you know he calls our church tree 'Charlie Brown'? I love that. I told him how Pastor Jay moved the tree and then it got hit but it saved people from getting run over. He thought that was cool. I think he's extra smart for only three, don't you?"

"Uh-huh."

"I think he's going to be jealous of the new baby, though, don't you? Don't you think Daughtry will be a good distraction? I'm going to tell Jocelyn I'll come get him every day after school and he can come over and play with Daughtry. See? Daughtry has a church job just like you and Pastor Jay. You're not mad, are you?"

Bethany smacked the wad of dough onto the floured spot between two rolling pins. "There's the crooked tree." She pointed at the metal cookie cutter she'd rescued from the garbage disposal in their Chicago apartment.

"Mom?"

She sliced the dough in quarters and handed a lump to Ava then pulled two cookie sheets from the space between the cupboards and fridge and turned on the oven.

"Why are you mad?" Tears choked the last word. "Daughtry doesn't ever have to come in our apartment and you don't ever have to do anything for him." Ava's fingers bit into the dough. "He'll protect me when I go outside and Pastor Jay loves him but you don't even care! You just don't want me to have anything I want ever!" The dough wad hit the rolling pin and bounced. Bethany caught it. Ava ran to her room and slammed the door.

Still cradling the ball of dough, Bethany dropped onto a chair. Muffled, discordant music seeped through the ceiling. Max's favorite Christmas album—the one with the tombstone on the cover. The "Carol of the Bells" sounded like a backdrop for a horror movie. It fit her mood.

Only a few minutes passed before Ava's door opened. Skinny arms slid around Bethany. She wrapped her daughter in a hug.

"I'm sorry." Ava pulled away, sniffed, and wiped her face on her sleeve. "Please don't be mad."

"I'm upset because"—*It's just one more thing I'll have to tear you away from if I take the job in St. Louis. And I'm ticked at Jay for getting involved in something that was none of his business.* "Because you and I should have talked this over privately."

"I know. I'm sorry. But it's kind of perfect, isn't it? He's our dog, but Pastor Jay is doing all the work." She giggled.

Bethany tucked a lock of tear-dampened hair behind Ava's ear. "It is not perfect. We can't let him do that. He's your dog and you need to take responsibility for him. You'll have to walk him every morning before school and as soon as you get home and before bed. And you'll have to carry a plastic bag and a pooper scooper every time and throw his poop away in the dumpster behind the church. It might sound fun now, but wait until February when it's five degrees out and the sidewalks aren't shoveled."

"I know." The smile hadn't dimmed. "I know all of that and I don't care. I'll do it. And I won't complain."

"We'll see about that." Bethany stretched her neck. She'd felt the headache coming on with the words "he could stay with me." Trapped. Again.

"Grandma says it's okay if you marry Pastor Jay."

"*What?*"

"She says you feel guilty that my dad died and you don't think you should be happy."

Bethany's hands tightened around the handles of the rolling pin. "What kind of a woman says things like that to a nine-year-old?" She punctuated her words by jabbing the rolling pin at the air. "You are not old enough to understand the—"

A knock at the door. A knock and a whine.

Chapter Twelve

"*D*aughtry!" Ava ran to the door and whipped it open. As she dropped to her knees, the man at the other end of the leash smiled. Apologetically?

"Hey, I hope I'm not interrupting anything."

Just the mother-daughter time I've looked forward to all week. "Do you need something?"

The smile that might have said I'm sorry stretched thin and disappeared. "They took Hank Spencer back to the hospital to replace his pacemaker. I promised Imogene I'd be there when he got out of surgery." He looked down at the puppy slobbering Ava's face. "Could you—I mean Ava—watch the dog?"

"And so it begins." Bethany turned away. Still gripping the rolling pin, she walked back to the table. "Sure. Why not?" She pressed the heel of her hand into the dough until one foot rose off the ground, eased up, then repeated the move. Press. Squish. She smoothed the edges, turned the glob over, and rammed it with the rolling pin. Roll. Turn. Roll harder. Turn. Press. Squish.

"Bethany."

She jumped at the touch of his hand on her shoulder. Her spine fused.

"Can we talk. I need to apologize for—"

"Ohhhh . . . a puppy!" Misty's breathy voice slipped in through the palpable tension.

Bethany turned, dislodging Jay's hand. "Hi!" Happy, happy smile. But Misty would read through it.

"Hi! Who's this?"

"This is Daughtry." Ava stood, wriggling dog in arms. "He's mine."

Misty's brows disappeared beneath green bangs. "Your mother let you get a dog?"

"Not exactly." Ava wrinkled her nose. "He's mine but he's staying with Pastor Jay."

"Ah. I see." Her smile said she thought she'd just been let in on a secret.

"Want to make cookies with us?" Bethany waved toward the table. A not-subtle way of telling the man with the dog he had indeed interrupted something.

Misty stepped over, pinched a bit of dough, and nodded approval. "Wish I could. I actually came to deliver some good/bad news."

Bring it on. What's a little more? "Okay . . .?"

"Jocelyn might be in labor."

"Yes!" Ava pumped the air with her fist. "We can have a real baby for the nativity."

Bethany felt her shoulders slump. *Figures.* "You can't go tonight."

"I'm so sorry."

"It's okay. I'll call my sis—"

"Pastor Jay"—Ava's face brightened, all trace of earlier tears and anger gone—"want to go to the Nutcracker with us tonight?"

"I'd love—" Jay grimaced. "It's up to your mom."

"Mom? Can he? It would be so fun!" Her petition took the same pitch as the earlier one. *Pleeease, pleeease can we keep the pastor, mom?*

"Who's going to watch the dog? You can't leave a puppy alone that long."

"I will." Misty raised her hand like a six-year-old. "I mean, we will. The whole house. Debbie is working tonight and she loves dogs and no one's allergic. Jerome will be ecstatic."

Once again, she had the minority opinion in a crowd of whiners. "Fine." Bethany stabbed the crooked tree cutter into the rolled out dough.

"So Pastor Jay can go with us?" Ava whirled in a tight circle.

"Sure." *Just don't expect me to talk to him.*

❄

Mood swings. Was that what he'd witnessed this afternoon? Jay cranked up the shower temperature until the air was white with steam and his skin bright red. *I can do all things through Christ who gives me strength.* He repeated the verse—once, and then again. But did the "all things" include understanding a pregnant woman?

He shouldn't have barged in on their plans. But the opportunity seemed an answer to prayer. If he had any hope of encouraging Bethany to rethink her decision, he had to have some contact with her. And what if Hoover was wrong about the time thing? What if she was on the verge of signing her baby away?

Towel wrapped around his waist, he walked into the bedroom. His bed looked like the church basement during a clothes drive. Sport jacket or dress shirt and sweater? Nobody wore ties anymore, did they? With snow in the forecast, the sweater was practical.

Snow. Up to three inches expected by 10 p.m. Maybe a foot by morning. That was his reason for going! He'd tell her he couldn't live with himself if he turned down Ava's invitation and they got stuck. A young girl and a pregnant, defenseless mom, stranded in downtown Milwaukee. He buttoned the shirt in front of the mirror. He was on his way to hero status once again.

❄

"You're going to wear your black dress, right?" Ava peered into the room, hair wrapped in a towel.

Bethany stood in front of her bedroom closet, hands on the doorframes. "I am not wearing the black dress. I am wearing the black pants and the gray sweater."

"Boring. Mom, this is a big deal. I heard kids talking about this in chorus way last month. Nobody could get tickets. I'm wearing the red lace Grandma got me at Nordstrom."

Grandma. She'd had just about all she could take of that woman's gifts. And opinions. "It's too cold for the red one."

"Duh. We'll only be outside for like seconds. Pastor Jay said he'd warm up his car before we come out."

"This is Wisconsin. We need to dress for what ifs."

"This is a date and you should be happy. You need to—" Ava's hand flew to her mouth, apparently stopped by the roiling emotion that was translating into some kind of terrifying expression on Bethany's face.

Bethany clamped her hands on her hips. "This is not a date and I am happy. I do not comprehend the thought process of a woman who can tell a nine-year-old her mother—"

"She didn't tell me. I heard her talking to Grandpa after they thought I was asleep. She wasn't being mean. I told her you liked Pastor Jay and she said that was good and I think it's better than good, so if everybody thinks it's—"

"Enough!" Bethany banged the folding doors of her closet and stood with her head down. "Go. Get. Dressed."

❄

She didn't feel guilty, did she? She'd been young and stupid and madly in love. And then suddenly she was alone and pregnant and terrified. But that dark, ugly time had brought her home and opened her eyes to God. And given her a baby with her daddy's eyes. *Rick, she has your eyes.*

Bethany slid onto the floor clutching the gray sweater and used it to mute her sobs. *I should have told you right away. I'm so sorry, Rick. Maybe if you'd known we were going to have a baby, you would have fought harder, your heart would have been stronger. I'm so sorry you've missed all of this. I'm sorry I . . .* The conviction hit like a deluge of ice water. *No more guilt. I'm a good mom and I'm doing a good job. Ava needs me.*

And it's okay to be happy.

She mopped her face and stood, leaving the damp and wrinkled gray sweater on the floor.

❄

Elizabeth checked her reflection in the vanity mirror as she sat in the cell phone parking lot at the airport. She'd needed a second coat of concealer to camouflage the dark circles under her eyes. Shannon said it was normal and she was probably only a matter of days away from leaving the nausea and exhaustion behind. But every pregnancy was different. How many times had she heard the girls at the store say that? Her phone dinged. *Just landed. See you in 15. Gate A.*

Like a teenager waiting for a blind date, she finger-combed her hair, straightened her necklace, and smoothed her blouse. She wanted to make a good first impression on this guy. The James she talked to on the phone this morning was the one she'd married eighteen years ago, not the James she'd lived with for the past five years. He'd told her for months now that if he got the promotion she'd see a changed man. The stress would be off and he could finally relax and enjoy life. But she knew this had little to do with a new office and a raise. This change was caused by the little person they'd meet tomorrow morning at 8:30.

Snow began to fall. Large flakes that floated straight down in the navy blue dusk. They stuck to the windshield and she studied their lacy uniqueness. No two alike. Like babies. She thought of the verse the man at the paint store had told her. *Knit together in*

111

my mother's womb. Tomorrow they might be able to find out if this fully formed little miracle was a Joy or a Joey. They'd count toes and analyze the slope of a miniscule nose. Would it turn up at the end like hers? Have a bump on top like James's?

She watched the clock. Thirteen minutes. Fourteen. She put the car in drive and pulled out of her lane. In less than a minute she spotted him, wheeling his bag through the sliding glass door, waving at her with a wrapped box. Green paper. Red bow. Too flat for toys. Which meant clothes.

She grinned as he strode closer. James had gone clothes shopping. She hoped the poor guy hadn't tried to find her size in the maternity section of some couture store. She didn't even know what size she wore. How do you shop for a body in constant flux? Must be baby clothes. Had he bought something pink? Or blue? No, he was smart enough to go neutral. She got out and gave him a hug. "Welcome home."

He kissed her. Not a quick brush of his lips. This was a kiss that said he wasn't just glad to come home. He was glad to come home to her. To them.

On the way to the restaurant they chit-chatted about the people he'd wined and dined at the lodge. She'd determined to let him lead. If he needed to ease into talking about the elephant in the car—the one she was sure wore pink booties—she'd give him space. Let him download and process his hectic week and tell her when he was ready to talk about the baby. She glanced at the package on the back seat. Perfect segue. Would he give it to her at dinner or make her wait for Christmas Eve?

She didn't have long to wait. The box accompanied them into the restaurant. When their server walked away, James asked why she'd ordered the house salad and grilled asparagus and nothing else. "Are you feeling okay?" He stroked her cheek. It seemed like years since she'd seen that tenderness in his eyes.

"Just a little queasy. It'll pass."

"You're probably just tired." He winked. "Maybe this will help." He bent, picked up the gift, and handed it to her. "A little something for Jamaica."

She gave him a quizzical look and tackled the ribbon. She wasn't one of those save-the-paper people. James took the wrapping and crumpled it into a ball. The name on the box made her pulse stutter. Neiman Marcus. She slid the top off the box. Tissue paper. So classy. She lifted the paper. A tag. Emelio Pucci. "You didn't . . ." She puckered and blew him an air kiss.

"Thought you needed something new and sexy for the trip."

She'd need everything new by February. And she very much doubted she'd be pulling off sexy in anything. "This is so sweet of—" The itty-bitty thing lying on the bed of pink would have looked great on her a month ago. A white one-piece swimsuit. One strap, backless, plunging V in front, tiny buckles up one side. She looked closer. Were they expandable? High fashion maternity? No. No room for growth. Even now, she couldn't fit her tummy or her becoming-more-womanly chest in this thing. "Is this . . . a joke?" She blinked back tears. He had to have spent more on this than on the football jersey she almost killed.

And then it hit her. He'd given her the wrong box. This one was meant for someone else. Another revelation slammed like a cement wall crashing down on her. *Hooked up with an old . . . what? Girlfriend?* Was Chris Wilson a she? Was all that sweet talk nothing but a cover-up? James was having an affair!

"A joke? What do you mean?"

She opened her mouth to confront him, but something else threatened to come out. She clamped her hand over her mouth and ran to the ladies' room.

When she walked back to the table, James was gone.

Chapter Thirteen

*J*ay stopped in front of Bethany's door and rubbed his damp palms on his jacket. This was ridiculous. It wasn't a date. And there'd be no opportunity for talk of any substance with Ava in the back seat. He knocked. Ava came to the door, wearing a red dress with matching shoes.

"Wow, aren't you pretty?"

"Thank you." She twirled. "You look pretty snazzy yourself."

"Snazzy? Isn't that word a bit outdated for such a hip girl?"

"Hip? Come on, Pastor Jay. I just read snazzy in a book." She arced one arm, hand over her head ballet-style. "I'll go see if Mom's ready." A look of something akin to fear crossed her face before she spun and glided toward the bedrooms. Not a good omen.

He grabbed a sugar cookie and took a bite. He was not going to be intimidated. He was the hero chauffeur tonight and he was going to enjoy himself no matter what.

And then Ava gasped. Jay winced. What was Bethany doing? Hiding in bed in her pajamas? And then—music to his ears—a giggle. Make that two. Bethany was laughing.

Ava danced out, stopped when she reached the kitchen, and curtseyed. "It is my pleasure to introduce to you the fierce, and *happy*, Bethany Schmidt."

The world stopped spinning, wavering a bit on its axis as Bethany entered the room. Black dress, covered in sparkles. Bare legs. Heels. More bling on her ears and hanging from a silver chain. The scent of wildflowers on a summer day permeated the air, blending with the sweet vanilla smell of fresh-baked cookies. An angel choir overshadowed the Christmas dirge coming from Max's apartment. The pink glow from the Christmas tree filled the room with ethereal light.

"Pastor Jay," Ava whispered. "I think you're supposed to say something." She nudged his elbow, dragging him back to the world of gravity and energy-saving light bulbs in an apartment building that smelled faintly of fried food and Max's patchouli. Still, a bit of a glow and an echo of "Hallelujah" remained.

"You are . . ." His mouth wouldn't sync with his brain.

Ava laughed. "Lovely? Gorgeous? Stunning?"

He nodded, and finally whispered, "All of the above."

"Thank you." Bethany looked directly at him and the earth slipped from its moorings once again.

"Wh-where's your coat?" Was he destined to stutter through the entire evening like a lovesick twelve-year-old?

Ava handed him Bethany's coat and he helped her into it, pulling her hair from under the collar and letting it float down in shimmering waves. He held out his hand for Ava's jacket and held it while she slipped into it. "Your carriage awaits, ladies." He looped Bethany's arm in his and lead the way through the falling snow to his eight-year-old tan Taurus—the pumpkin that had not, as he'd hoped, turned into a coach.

❄

The Land of Sweets. Ladyfinger mountains covered in whipped cream snow. Shimmering, glazed flowers. Bethany leaned forward in her seat, awaiting the arrival of the Sugar Plum Fairy. And there she was, dressed in white, a tiny crown on her head, her skirt standing out from her body like frosted daisy petals. She bowed and dipped, spun in dizzying pirouettes, every move graceful and perfect.

Trumpets and castanets set the fandango rhythm that transformed into an Arabian melody as two dark-skinned men and a woman moved lithely in unison across the stage, wispy veils trailing. As the Russian dolls entered, Ava grabbed her hand. And Jay took the other, yanking her out of the magic.

How had she lost the battle to put Ava between them? And did she really care? His hand was warm, strong. Safe. She didn't pull away as the flowers danced beneath a crystal dewdrop and the handsome cavalier lured the Sugar Plum Fairy to the center of the floor and the atmosphere hummed with the fluid notes of the Nutcracker Suite as they waltzed, lighter than air.

And then Clara was asleep beneath the dazzling gold and white tree, cradling the nutcracker in her arms. And Bethany and Jay and Ava were on their feet, clapping.

"Mom, that was the best! I want to take ballet again. Please?"

"I want to go to the Purple Door again. Please?" Jay's fingers entwined with hers.

The theater was still dark. No need to pull away. And no point in resisting the pleading. Again. "Maybe to ballet and yes to the Purple Door."

Jay left them in the foyer and went to get the car. Bethany checked her phone. No word from Misty.

Ava sighed dreamily. "Wasn't this the best night ever? And there's still ice cream—or chocolate sorbet for some people. Don't you sometimes just want time to stop and an hour to last forever? I would pick this one. What would you pick?"

Bethany hugged her. "This one. And the one where I saw you for the very first time. And every one in between."

"Yeah, I guess me too." Her eyes lit with mischief. "But this one includes the part where you and Pastor Jay were holding hands in the dark."

Pressing her shoulder against Ava's, Bethany gave in to laughter. "I'll keep this one too." *Because Grandma is right. I did feel guilty. Not for having you, but for getting to know you and love you when your daddy never had the chance.*

It was time to give herself permission to be happy.

❄

"Isn't this the best? Just the three of us?" Ava wiped peppermint ice cream off her mouth with the back of her hand.

Kind of like a family. Jay caught himself before saying the words out loud. He needed a more subtle way to engage Ava in his plan.

"Do you want to have kids someday, Pastor Jay?"

Or maybe he didn't. Evidently God was taking it from here.

Bethany coughed on her chocolate sorbet. Jay hid his smile behind two scoops of pumpkin spice. "Yes, I do. Families are very important." When Ava only grinned an answer, he decided to expand on his. "I told you I pretty much grew up without a family. So I did a lot of daydreaming when I was your age. I pretended I lived on a farm with a huge yard and lots of animals. But my favorite part of the dream was my three brothers and two sisters."

"I do that too sometimes. I imagine Mom gets married and has lots of kids and I'm the oldest so I get to take care of all of them."

Jay glanced at Bethany. She'd picked up her phone and was trying to look like she wasn't listening. "Where would you want to live if that happened? In the country? In a neighborhood where you could ride a bike?"

Bethany looked up. The tilt of her head and cute little sucking noise she made between tight lips told her he'd crossed the line.

117

"I don't ever want to live anywhere but where we are. I already figured it out that we could turn two apartments into one so we could have more bedrooms and a bigger kitchen and we would have to get a van instead of our—"

"Well,"—Jay put an end to Ava's imaginings just as Bethany kicked his shin under the table—"it's fun to dream, but it's more important that we learn to be content where God puts us. Sometimes we think we want something different than what we have, but if we just change the way we look at things and start counting our blessings we find out we're really in the right place with the right people after all."

Ava laughed. "You're preaching, Pastor Jay."

"I guess that's just who I am." He grinned and turned his full focus on Bethany. "Just a poor preacher who wants us all to be like the Apostle Paul who said, 'I have learned, in whatsoever *state* I am, therewith to be content.'" *As in content in pregnant, going-to-be-a-mom-again state.* He wrinkled his nose Bethanyesque and she copied him, finally breaking into a smile.

❄

Subtle, Pastor Jay. Whatsoever *state* I'm in. *Cute.* He might as well have said, "I have learned to be content in Wisconsin."

At the moment she was. Or she had been before the "wish I had a ton of brothers and sisters" conversation started. Jay was thirty-four. In a normal relationship, they'd probably date for a few more months and then he'd propose. At their age, what was the point of a long engagement? They'd get married soon, maybe next fall. Except, if all went according to plan, she'd be looking like the Stay Puft Marshmallow Man if she donned a wedding dress next fall. And if the first egg transfer didn't work, they'd agreed to try for a year. What if she didn't get pregnant before next January? The earliest they could get married would be Christmas, two years from now. If, by some miracle, he wanted to get married earlier, he'd have to undergo testing and there would be limits put on—she blushed—the part of marriage a man looks forward to the most. *Lord, help!*

❄

Ava fell asleep on the way home. The windshield wipers swiped a clear arc on the window, but it filled almost as quickly. Jay set the wipers up a notch then took off his gloves and slid his hand across the console, covering Bethany's. "Thank you for letting me come."

"I'm glad you did." Her nose wrinkled. "I'd sure hate to be driving in this."

"So that's all I am to you. A chauffeur?"

"Oh, maybe a little more than that."

"Suppose I'll have to be satisfied with that. For now." He kept his gaze on the road, but he was sure she smiled.

"Jay, there's something I need to talk to you about."

"I know." He tipped his head toward the back seat. "Now's probably not a good time."

"No. Now's not a good time."

"Maybe tomorrow sometime?"

She rubbed the back of her neck. Was he pressing too hard? He didn't want to spoil the night. "Or whenever."

She seemed to relax at that. He smiled at her, an attempt to soften her mood even more. "Can I just say one thing?"

"I guess."

"I don't really have the right to ask, but I'd be grateful if you gave me the chance to say what I want to say before you make your final decision."

She was quiet so long he wondered if she was sleeping. "Okay. I can do that."

"Decision about what?" Ava sat up and yawned. "What are you guys talking about?"

"Nothing." They said it in unison.

"Uh-huh. I bet I know. And I say go for it!"

Bethany shook her head. "Go back to sleep, Ava."

They rode in silence the rest of the way. The snow seemed wetter and heavier as they neared home. Ice clumped on the wipers. At a stoplight, Jay opened the window, reached out, and snapped the blade, dislodging a glob of packed snow. "Almost there," he said, as much to himself as Bethany.

"You're a good driver."

"Thanks." He imagined most heroes didn't blush like he knew he was. Or maybe that was why a lot of them did their good deeds under cover of darkness.

He didn't fully exhale until they drove into the parking lot between the church and the Enterprise. He pulled up and told Bethany to wait while he unlocked the building. Then he turned and walked back to her, letting the next few minutes play out in his head the way they probably wouldn't. He opened Bethany's door. "Hate to wake Sleeping Beauty. I suppose she's too old for me to carry her."

"She'll think she is." Bethany got out, closed her door and leaned against it. Snowflakes landed on her eyelashes and dotted her hair. "Thank you for a wonderful evening."

He held her eyes. "I know we have things to straighten out, but can we just pretend for a minute that everything's good between us?"

She nodded.

"And can I pretend for a minute that it's okay if I kiss you?"

Another nod. He stepped closer, put his hands on her shoulders, and leaned in. Could a moment be more magical? The warmth of her lips, the smell of her, falling snow deadening all sound but the cadence of his pulse and—

"Yes! That's what I'm talking about!" Ava fist pumped through the open window, then she closed it, got out, and ran inside the building, laughing like a hyena.

❄

"When Ashley's mom got remarried she was really mad." Ava talked around her toothbrush.

Bethany peeked out from under her washcloth. "Where is this leading?"

"To us. To happily ever after. Ashley's therapist said she had to adjust her thinking to accept two dads, but it will be totally different for me since I don't already have a dad, it's just all good, isn't it?"

Bethany hid behind the washcloth, wishing she could stay there, lingering in the warmth of a sweet memory. But there would be no lingering with a now-wide-awake amateur psychologist at her elbow. "It was just a kiss, Ava." *One you were not supposed to see.*

"That was not 'just' a kiss, Mom. I've seen ordinary kissing and that was different."

"Ordinary kissing?" Did she really want to dissect this at eleven o'clock at night?

"Ashley and Kevin kissed and Emma S. and Caleb kissed all the time before they broke up."

"You're nine! That's disgusting. And dumb. You do know that, right? You know that a kiss isn't a casual thing, it's something you save for someone"—she'd walked right into this one—"special."

"My point exactly. It's stupid when fourth graders kiss. I have never kissed a boy, Mom, ever, and I won't until I'm really, really in love. Like when I'm fourteen at least."

"Eighteen at least."

"Whatever. You're changing the subject."

"The subject at the moment is rinse your mouth and get in bed."

"Admit you like him."

"I like him. But that doesn't mean we're—" A cold, wet fingertip sealed her lips.

121

"Shh. Go to bed and dream of him." Ava planted a loud kiss on her cheek. "Dream about the three of us."

❄

A funnel cloud of pink snowflakes whirled around her. The wind howled and whipped her hair into her eyes. Bethany stood in the middle of the dark intersection in a white lace dress, calling for Jay. "We can't get married until I tell you—"

"Bethany! I'll fix it. I'm getting your chocolate sorbet."

"No! Not now! I have to—"

Bawk! A chicken landed on her head. Jay's laughter blended with the howling wind.

"Jay, listen to me. I have to—"

"Mom! Wake up!"

Bethany jolted upright and lifted the covers for Ava to crawl in. "You won't believe the dream I had." She started to laugh. "I was outside and the wind was—" The howling started up again. A shiver skittered up her spine. The noise grew louder then suddenly stopped.

Not wind. Sirens.

Chapter Fourteen

ethany jumped out of bed. Ava folded her hands on her knees. "Please God, take care of whoever they're going to help and protect the firefighters or EMTs and—"

The phone vibrated on the nightstand. Ava grabbed it. "It's Misty." Fear roughened her voice.

Bethany punched the speaker phone button. "Misty, what is it?"

"The roof caved in." She teetered on the edge of hysteria. "The flat part. It just . . . crashed. It was so loud and it shook the house but we're all fine. We're outside. Can you open the church?"

"Come to my apartment. All of you."

"Okay. Good. We're coming."

"Get dressed, Ava, and find all the blankets you can and heat some water in the tea pot." She grabbed a pair of jeans off a chair, stepped into them as she walked then pulled the gray sweater over her head as she sprinted toward the kitchen, flipping lights on as she went.

She ran down the hall. Red and white light strobed through the sidelight at the end. Snow plastered the narrow window. She unlocked the door.

Steps pounded on the stairs. "Bethany? What happened?" Jay leaped over the last two steps. He wore shorts and a rumpled white T-shirt.

"The roof collapsed at Serenity. They're all okay. Misty's bringing everyone over."

Looking dazed and adorable, he rubbed the dark shadow on his chin. "I'll get dressed."

The door opened and snow flew in with Misty, carrying a sleeping Jerome. Jocelyn walked heavily behind them, followed by Debbie and Kathleen, and Crystal carrying baby Riley.

"Jocelyn, take everyone to my apartment."

"We"—Misty leaned against the door—"ran out in bare feet. I went back in and got boots and coats. The whole downstairs is . . . a mess. Plaster and dirt and snow. What if the whole house falls down? What if we can't get back in? Where are we going to stay?"

"Right here." Bethany hugged her. "I thought you'd be at the hospital by now."

"Her contractions were eight minutes apart around nine, then stopped."

"Come on, let's get you warm."

Jay bounded down the steps again. "Misty." He hugged her and Jerome. "Thank God everyone's all right. What do you need?"

"Now that we're all in and warm, nothing."

Bethany counted on her fingers. "As far as I can figure, there are ten beds and eight couches in this building and we only need beds for seventeen of us. We just need to do a bit of a Chinese fire drill."

"Good math." Jay winked. "Looks like you've got things under control." He zipped his jacket and pulled a stocking cap from his pocket. "I'm going to check out the damage." As he walked out, he pointed at Bethany and looked at Misty. "Just don't let her overdo it."

"What was that all about? I just went through a near death experience and I'm supposed to be coddling you?"

"I think he's just a bit of a chauvinist. In a good way. He's taking care of me. I could get used to that."

A guttural sound came from Misty's throat. "Envy's a sin, huh?"

"Yep. Sorry."

"Fine. Let's go wake some people up."

❄

Jay stood on the sidewalk in front of the Enterprise. It was as close as they'd let him get. An ambulance, firetruck, and two squad cars blocked most of his view, but he'd seen enough to know that half of the living room had caved in.

"Jay!" Bernard half-sprinted through the snow and stood beside him without saying another word.

Hoover and Max joined them. The four men stood in silence as the emergency vehicles pulled away. Bernard clapped his gloved hands together. "Well, better assemble the troops. If we can just get it boarded up tonight, we can assess the extent of the damage in the morning."

Jay nodded. "This isn't going to be cheap."

"Kick me if I say something about a pound of prevention."

"I've had the same thoughts. There just wasn't any way we could have fit this in the budget."

"God will bring good out of this." Hoover looked up toward the street light.

"I hope so." Jay's cheeks puffed out as he let his breath out slowly. He noticed Hoover's half smile. "Hey, even pastors have faith crises."

"Understandable." Hoover brushed snow from his face but continued looking up. "Do you have people who can do the reconstruction work?"

Bernard huffed. "We have people who will work. But I wouldn't know where to start. I think we'll have to hire this out."

"I know some guys," Hoover said.

Bernard pulled out his phone. "Insurance will cover some of it. Pretty sure not enough. I don't know what we can afford to pay."

"No worries. They won't ask for money. Just a place to stay and a few hot meals. I could have five of them here by morning. At least."

Bernard swiveled to face Hoover. Jay and Max did the same. "You could have five guys who work pro bono here two days before Christmas?"

"Yep." Face still turned into the falling snow, Hoover winked. "I'll go make some calls."

"Strange guy." Bernard stuck his phone back in his pocket. "You trust him?"

"I do."

"Where's he from?" Max asked.

Jay's gaze followed Hoover until the darkness and swirling snow camouflaged him. "I have no idea."

Bethany dug through the storeroom at the Enterprise where they kept clothes and linens "just in case." She filled a wicker basket with sheets and towels and disposable diapers.

Ava ran in, breathless but glowing. "Can you find sweats that would fit Jocelyn? She's afraid she'll have to go to the hospital tonight and she's only got her nightgown."

"Better hope she doesn't go into real labor before the plows come through." Jay stood behind Ava. "The roads are a mess. Has to be at least eight inches so far."

126

Ava ran out of the room, leaving Bethany alone with a man who looked in need of a reassuring hug. She put the basket on her hip and walked over to him.

"You shouldn't be carrying this." He took the basket.

"How does it look?"

"Not good. Your dad's out there talking to the fire chief. Then he and I and Max and Hoover and a couple of the deacons will get it boarded up to keep the snow out."

"How long do you think the reconstruction will take?" Things were going smoothly so far, but how long would peace reign now that everyone's routine was disrupted?

"A week or two, I imagine, although Hoover says he can have a work crew here by morning."

"From where?"

"I have no idea. But we'll need to house them."

She laughed. And then she started planning. "We can bring beds from Serenity and set them up in the basement. If the mattresses can't be used, we'll ask church people to bring air mattresses."

"That'll work. You're a genius."

"You always wanted a big family. Now you have lots and lots of brothers and sisters. And a dog. And a chicken."

"And a best friend." He pulled her close in what did not feel at all like a best friend's hug.

❄

By four in the morning, the room shuffle was complete. She and Ava had given their apartment to Jocelyn, Jerome, and Misty. Max had moved to Jay's hide-a-bed. Kathleen was bunking with Sandy and Shellianne with Debbie. Tark was in Hoover's spare room and Crystal and baby Riley had Tark's apartment. Only Vienna and her daughter were untouched by making room in the inn.

Bethany stood in the kitchen of Max's apartment, surveying her temporary digs. Black walls, black carpet. Six-foot-tall speakers. But in the midst of the darkness there were pinpoints of light, signs of Max's transformation. A fuzzy white pillow on the couch, a miniature Christmas tree. Pictures of the kids he now saw on weekends covered the refrigerator. And the only thing on the glass-topped black cubes he used as a coffee table was a Bible.

"We did it." She smiled as Ava yawned. "Go to bed."

"It's scary in there."

"But it's clean." That was more than she could say about the condition of Tark's apartment before Debbie and Misty tackled it to make it livable for Crystal and Riley. "Fresh sheets on the bed."

"*Black* sheets."

"Better us than a three-year-old and his ten-month-pregnant mom. I'll put on some music to lull you to sleep. How about a little Leper or Dark Valentine?" Christian goth. She hadn't understood it as a kid in the nineties. It made even less sense now. But there was no arguing with the fact that Max could talk to people who wouldn't have looked twice at the rest of them.

"Good night, mom. Put some headphones on before you start head banging." Ava gave a tired wave and headed down the hall to the black-sheeted king size bed they'd be sharing for as long as it took to make Serenity livable.

A faint tap at the door startled her. "Who is it?" There was no chance it would be a stranger, but the night that started with a bizarre dream and ended in a black-walled kitchen had her jumpy.

"Jay."

She let him in. "Don't take this personal, but you look awful." She gestured to the lacquered black kitchen table. "Have a seat. Coffee?"

"Decaf if there is any. Can't imagine Max drinking anything that wimpy." He sat back in the chair and closed his eyes.

Bethany found a jar of instant decaf. She didn't let herself look at the expiration date. She put a mug in the microwave and walked over to him. "Did you get it done?" She picked a bit of pink insulation out of his hair.

He nodded. "It's going to be a bigger job than we first thought. For one thing, the whole house will have to be rewired to meet code. And we'll have to add insulation. The list is ridiculous."

The microwave dinged. She fixed the coffee and set it in front of him along with two doughnuts she'd found in a box on the counter. "We did good tonight. I felt bad you guys had to be out in the cold. It was almost like a party in here. We worked together like a family. Nobody complained. Not once." She explained her logic behind the room assignments. "I told everyone to bring what they have to the church by eight and we'll all have breakfast together." She leaned against the counter, massaging the taut muscles in her low back.

"Good plan. You're in your element with something like this."

He was right. There was something energizing about helping people help each other. Exactly the kind of thing she'd be doing in St. Louis.

"Your back hurting?"

"A bit. If my calculations are right, Ava and I changed sheets on seven beds."

"You shouldn't be doing so much." He got up, arranged two kitchen chairs, walked to the living room, and came back with the fuzzy white pillow. "Put your feet up."

"I don't need—"

"Now. Your ankles are going to swell."

She narrowed her eyes at him. "You're weird." She sat down, welcoming the pillow behind her back and the weight off her feet. "Thank you. But this is a good kind of tired. Tonight was fun." She pulled his second doughnut apart, took a small piece and stuck it in her mouth, and tried to chew around a yawn. "It doesn't look like we'll get much chance to talk today, so maybe we should get a few things cleared up now." She yawned again.

"The only thing you should do now is go to bed. I'll take my coffee to go." He stood and kneeled beside her. "Can we put everything on hold until after the weekend?"

She leaned into his arms. "I think so." She was too tired to listen to the little voice that said the longer she put this off, the harder it would be.

He didn't kiss her. He just held her, rocking ever so slightly back and forth. And then he brushed his lips across her forehead. "Tell me to go home."

So tempting to imagine a time when he wouldn't have to leave. "Go home." It came out so soft she wondered if he'd heard.

"Walk me to the door."

He made it to the hallway, then leaned in for a kiss on the lips. She had the door half closed when he held up one finger. "You know how I said you were in your element tonight?"

"Yes."

"You should be doing this full-time."

"Jay." Had he really not heard her when she said she wasn't taking the job?

"I was going to wait to tell you when we had that talk we never get around to having, but"—he smiled in a way she could only label hopeful—"the board voted unanimously on Thursday night to offer you the newly created position of Community Coordinator. Meaning you'd be overseeing Serenity and the Enterprise, which you are clearly already doing. It wouldn't mean a huge raise, but hopefully more down the road."

"That would be incredible if "—*you don't turn your back on me when I tell you about the surrogacy*—"everything else . . . falls into place." But wasn't this the best of everything? The kind of job she'd dreamed of without uprooting Ava? Wasn't this an answer to prayer—even if it meant working around awkwardness with Jay? They'd been co-workers before they were friends. Couldn't mature adults find their way back to that? "No. Yes. I mean no 'if'—my answer is yes."

Smile lines splayed from the corners of his eyes. Still holding her gaze, he backed toward his apartment.

"Bethany! Jay!" Misty sounded more frantic than she had three hours earlier. "Jocelyn's baby is coming *now*!"

Chapter Fifteen

"*B*oil water!" Misty hovered over Jocelyn who lay propped on pillows on Bethany's couch. Ava kneeled beside her.

"Isn't that what they say to keep nervous fathers busy?"

"In this case it's to give you something to do so you quit fidgeting." Misty laughed. "And I want to give her raspberry tea right after birth."

Bethany walked from the stove to the sink and back to the stove. "Shouldn't Jay be back here by now?"

"My kit's probably under a foot of debris."

"Are you sure it isn't dangerous? Should I go check—"

The door opened a crack. "I'll just leave this right here." Jay's arm appeared, pushing Misty's midwife kit. "Text if you need anything."

"Chicken!"

"You got that right," he called through the door. "Me and Esther will be hangin' out upstairs."

Jocelyn groaned.

Misty pulled back the sheet. "She's crowning."

Bethany was about to ask again if she should send Ava next door. Debbie had taken Jerome to Shellianne's the moment they knew it was active labor. But the thought dissipated as she watched Ava turn over the cloth she placed on Jocelyn's head. The girl was as calm as her mother was anxious.

"Try not to push for just a second. Come breathe with her, Bethany."

Finally, something constructive. She kneeled beside Jocelyn, took her hand, and began pant-blowing as if it hadn't been nine years since the last time she'd used Lamaze. *He-he-hoo-hoo.* Jocelyn copied her rhythm, at one with every woman who had given birth before her. And then the air was filled with the lusty cry of a baby girl.

Tears in her eyes, Jocelyn reached out for her daughter. "Noelle," she whispered.

"Perfect name." Misty wrapped mom and baby together, skin to skin.

Ava crouched next to Bethany and tentatively touched one small pinking foot. "Mom, this is the best. When you have a baby for—" Ava covered her mouth with her hand and winked. "When you have another baby, I'm going to be there to help, right?"

Bethany swiped at tears and put her arm around her daughter. "I couldn't do it without you."

❄

A sleep-deprived but joyful crowd gathered for breakfast in the church basement. They'd moved Jocelyn and baby Noelle to Bethany's room around dawn. Mom, baby, and Misty were all sound asleep when Bethany checked on them. Bethany cracked an egg in each hand and scanned the room for Jay. Again. The poor guy had to be exhausted. Still, it wasn't like him to not show.

At the counter next to her, Max opened a package of bacon. "I see you found my stash," he said.

"Four pounds in the freezer, two in the fridge." She smiled at the guy with the spread-wing vampire bat tattooed on his forearm. "You're a regular carnivore."

"If God didn't want us to eat animals, why did he make them out of meat?"

Shellianne laughed. It was no secret she had a crazy crush on Max. To his credit, he was keeping his distance in hopes of being reconciled to his ex-wife.

Crystal had strapped Riley to her back and was busy making hash browns out of the potatoes she collected on her door-to-door hunt at the Enterprise. "What a sweet, motley crew," she said.

Hoover walked into the kitchen. "I've got six more hungry hippos out there. What can I do to help?"

"Six more?"

"Yeah, Jasper's wife's an electrician so she came along."

"Where did you find these guys?"

"Oh, here and there. Used to bike with them back in the day, before they all went and got jobs and kids."

Do you have children, Hoover? She'd known him for a week and knew nothing about him. "First batch of bacon and eggs is done." Bethany spooned eggs into a bowl and pointed at a platter of bacon. "If you want to carry these out and come back for toast and hash browns, I'll bring coffee. We'll feed your crew first."

As she handed the bowl to Hoover, Jerome rushed in and wrapped his arms around her knees. "Noelle is borned! Did you thee her Bethany?"

She bent down to his eye level. "Isn't she the most beautiful baby in the world?"

"Yeth. In the whole wide world!" He turned and ran smack into Jay, who scooped him up, gave him a high five, and sent him on his way.

"Good morning, sleepyhead." She smoothed the hair sticking out straight above Jay's ear.

"Can't be morning yet. Did you get any sleep?"

"A little."

"Promise me you'll take a nap."

"I promise."

Jay looked from side to side as if he had something to say to her alone. "Must have been amazing for you—watching a baby come into this world."

"It was. I know why Misty became a midwife. We witnessed a miracle this morning."

He appeared ready to speak, then hesitated and started again. "Doesn't it make you want to change your mind?"

"About what?" The dread creeping up her spine told her she didn't need to ask.

"About carrying a baby to term and then giving it to someone else?"

Jay knew about the IVF. How? "Jay, can we talk about this when we can be alone?"

"About you changing your mind?"

"No. I can't do that."

"Then we don't need to talk." He turned and walked out of the kitchen.

❄

Elizabeth stumbled to the bathroom on Friday morning and leaned on the sink, staring at purple circles under her eyes and hair that looked like it had been styled with a hand mixer. After hours of ignoring James's calls, she'd finally fallen asleep sometime around two, only to wake again at five for another round of sobbing. She hadn't set her alarm, but the snowplow woke her moments ago. It was seven forty-five and her appointment was at 8:30. She brushed her teeth, took a five-minute shower, and headed for the car. But when she opened the garage door, a strange SUV blocked her way.

James got out, looking in worse shape than she did. "Elizabeth, what in tarnation is going on? Where did you go last night?"

"Where did *you* go last night?"

"I ran after you but you weren't in the car so I came back in and called you and looked all over. This is insane and you're scaring me. You didn't make any sense last night. I buy you an expensive gift and you go ballistic? All you've talked about for months is getting in shape for vacation. You worked hard for that beach bod. Don't you want to show it off?"

"Are you serious? This 'beach bod' is going to look like a beached whale in February!"

"What do you mean? Is something wrong? Are you sick? You've been so tired lately and not eating right and acting—"

"Of course I'm sick! I'm three months pregnant!"

The neighbor shoveling his sidewalk stopped and stared.

"You're *what*?"

She glared at him, tilted her head. He looked so flat-out sincere. If she didn't know better . . . "Wait. You didn't know?"

"How would I know? You didn't say a word until this minute."

"But Linda from Dr. Mae's office called you. Last Friday, when Mom was in the ER."

He shook his head as if trying to wake from a dream. "Nobody called. Did you honestly believe I knew all this time?"

Tears crested her bottom lids and dripped onto the freshly plowed drive. "When you made such a big deal out of dinner that night . . . the wine and . . . and . . ."

"Oh, honey . . . I was just celebrating the promotion. Oh my gosh. You must think I'm a complete jerk. You poor . . . you're pregnant? We're pregnant?" His eyes misted and he wrapped her in his arms.

She leaned into him, sobbing all over his coat. "I th-thought you weren't happy, that you didn't want to be a f-father. And th-then I thought Chris was a woman and you were having an affair."

"Oh, baby, I would never, ever do that to us. I couldn't be happier. And with this new job, I won't need to travel as much and"—laughter rumbled in his chest—"we can fly to Denver or New York for a weekend in January to exchange that suit for one more . . . accommodating."

"There's a N-Neiman Marcus in Northbrook."

"Illinois? Not exotic enough for my pregnant wife."

And then James, her what-will-people-think husband, dipped her back and kissed her like she'd never been kissed before. When he righted her, he waved at the gaping neighbor. "Hey, George! Guess what? We're pregnant!"

❄

Elizabeth squeezed James's hand as they watched the grainy, black-and-white image on the screen. "Look at that nose. I think it's yours."

The ultrasound technician printed out a copy. "You'll get to see that little nose in person right around the Fourth of July."

James laughed. "Figured we'd have a firecracker after the ruckus it's caused already."

"Okay, I'm about 90 percent sure about this, but there's some room for error this early. Do you want me to tell you what I think—"

"Yes!" They answered together.

"Anyone want to venture a guess?" The technician held the wand suspended over Elizabeth's belly as she waited.

"A girl." Again, their answers came in duet.

"Well . . . as it so happens . . . you are both . . . according to what I'm seeing right here . . ." She rolled the wand across Elizabeth's skin then stopped and pointed at the screen. "Wrong."

Elizabeth drew James's hand to her lips and kissed it. "I've been wrong about a lot this week. But this one I won't apologize for."

Becky Melby

"Me neither." He puffed out his chest. "I'm going to have a son."

They walked out to the front desk holding hands. Linda grinned at them. "Well?"

"It's a boy."

"Congratulations! Did you get a video of the phone call?"

Elizabeth grimaced. "I think you might have gotten too busy last Friday and forgot to call." She turned to James with a tiny smirk that said, "If she only knew."

Linda looked at James. "One of our externs made calls for me that day. And I know she called you. She made a point of saying how shocked you were and how you said it must be a . . . wrong number." She grimaced. "Oh my."

"Wow." James shook his head and laughed. "That could have messed up someone's life big time." He winked at Elizabeth. "Miscommunication will do that."

❄

Jay jabbed the shingle ripper beneath another brittle chunk of asphalt. His back ached and he'd bruised the side of his hand, but physical pain seemed to take the edge off the hurt inside.

The laughter of Hoover and his buddies seemed far away, as if he stood behind a wall of glass, just observing. Separate. Again.

Was he wrong to not just accept Bethany's decision? He'd supported Alexandra and another woman from Serenity when they chose to make adoption plans for their babies. He'd commended them on their selflessness. Why couldn't he see Bethany's decision in the same light?

Because her choice wasn't based on what was best for her child.

Because he knew what it felt like to be rejected by your mother because you were an inconvenience.

Bethany was a loving, capable mother. Sure, she didn't make a lot of money, but she wasn't a material girl. How many times had he heard her comment about the fun of buying everything second hand? And she wasn't lacking in support. Her dad was more supportive of his pregnant-out-of-wedlock daughter than Jay ever would have imagined. What was her deal?

He'd been sure the job the elder board had created just for her would change Bethany's mind. It wasn't his place to offer it to her, that was the board's responsibility. And given the cost of reconstructing Serenity, they'd have to renege.

But he'd made up his mind he'd give up half his salary if it meant making Bethany feel secure enough to give up the ridiculous idea of adoption.

❄

Bethany showered in a gray-tiled bathroom and dried with a black towel. She'd sent Ava to bed after lunch and promised Jay and Misty she'd take a nap before the program, but she couldn't imagine falling asleep. She had two hours until she had to put on her Mary costume and pretend to be the mother of Jesus, a woman who was probably deeply in love with a man who had willingly agreed to stand by her side come-what-may. Two hours until she had to hold Jay's hands, look into his eyes, and sing, "We can't do this on our own." *Lord, I can't do this.*

She stretched out on black sheets next to Ava and stared at the silver cross Max had painted on his bedroom wall—"To remember what Jesus did for me." She tried to pray, but couldn't get beyond "I can't." If Jay, the most understanding, compassionate man she knew, had such an intense reaction to her having a baby for her sister, what would the rest of the neighborhood say? Her dad was thrilled at the prospect of Sarah's dreams finally being realized, but had he thought it through enough to realize he might have to ask her to leave her job because of the controversy? And whose idea was it to create the Community Coordinator job? Jay's? Just to keep her here? But the meeting was on Thursday and he hadn't intercepted the call from Dr. Morganstein until Friday.

She'd thought they could go back to being friends and still work together, but the way he'd looked at her this morning told her that was impossible. There was probably no point in even thinking about it, since the repairs to Serenity would eat up any funds they may have set aside for this made-up job. She rubbed her temple and tried to relax the tension tightening like a steel band around her head.

Maybe she'd be doing them all a favor by just resigning quietly. Quietly. The way the Bible said Joseph was going to end his betrothal to Mary. But that was before the angel talked to him and told him not to be afraid to take her as his wife. Where was an angel when a person really needed one?

Exhaustion finally won out and she fell asleep. When she woke, Ava was curled next to her. Late afternoon light slanted through black blinds, painting stripes on the walls. Prison bars. She thought back to Misty's flippant comment about knocking down the bars and going with the guy. But the bars weren't hers to destroy.

Whether she'd be free to stay or forced to move was all up to Jay.

Chapter Sixteen

J ames kneeled in front of the Christmas tree. One hand rocked the Rudolph Red cradle that still smelled of fresh paint. The other hand touched a popsicle stick stable he'd made in kindergarten. The news was on, but he'd turned the volume down and for once wasn't glued to the TV. "This is amazing. Like a scene right out of *It's a Wonderful Life*."

James had watched the movie and never told her? Who was this guy? "I never realized before how cold and sterile I'd made it."

He pulled her to him. "I told you I had a lot of time to reflect this week. I had time to think about us too."

"When you weren't doing happy hour with Chris." She stuck her tongue out at him. "Have I mentioned I'm sorry I overreacted?"

"Is that what you call it?" He laughed and nuzzled his face in her hair. "Don't you know it's rude to interrupt an apology with an apology? I have told you approximately twenty-three times you're forgiven. Anyway, as I was trying to say, if there was coldness in our Christmases the past few years, I think I've been to blame. I told myself everything I did was for you, for us, but so much of it has been about me. About proving something. I don't want to live like that. Especially now. We've got a little guy to think about."

She sank into him, wanting to freeze-frame this moment, but when she looked up to kiss him, she noticed a familiar face on TV. "I know him." She grabbed the remote and turned up the sound.

"... it's just what we do. God's people help each other."

"That's Hoover, from the paint store."

"... why I'd like to put a call out to other believers and kind-hearted people in this town to pitch in and help Bethlehem Community Church rebuild Serenity. If at all possible, we'd like to get these moms and their children back in their home by Sunday, with presents under a brand new Christmas tree."

"Thank you, Mr. Hoover." The reporter turned to the camera. "There's a number at the bottom of your screen if you'd like to offer to help or find out what building supplies are still needed to rebuild after the roof collapsed. And if you'd like to come out and meet some of these wonderful, resilient people, come on out for their Christmas program at 6:30 tonight. Next let's . . ."

"You have to help them." Elizabeth stood up. "They need building supplies. And a Christmas tree. *We* have to help them!"

"Who is that guy and how do you know him?"

"I'll tell you on the way." And she'd text Shannon on the way.

"This is for real? Not some figment of your pregnant imagination?" James ducked as a star-shaped pillow flew at his head. "Fine. Anything you say, little mama. Let's go."

❄

"We need to move to the basement." Yolanda waved her script over the crowd of angels and shepherds in the side room. "They need this room for seating."

From a distance, Bethany watched Jay's face as the shock registered. They'd never used the overflow room for anything but storage.

"Bethy, can you help get everyone moving?" Her dad gave her a quick, one-armed hug. "They're lined up out on the sidewalk."

"'They' who?"

"People. From all over the city. They saw Hoover on the news."

"Hoover was on the news?" Not waiting for an answer, she ushered MacKenzie, Destiny, Lena and a gaggle of whispering girls down the stairs.

MacKenzie grabbed her elbow. "I tried to tell them to shut up, Bethany. But they're telling everybody."

"Telling them what?"

"That you're pregnant."

Bethany gripped the handrail. "I'm not pregnant."

"But Destiny heard Pastor Jay say you were."

"I'll explain that later. But I'm not pregnant."

"But *every*body thinks you are. The whole church—"

"Miss Bethany, Pastor Jay!" Hoover waved from the top of the stairs, calling into the crowd.

"Down here." Jay pushed upstream toward her. She was pinned against the wall. Trapped.

By the time Hoover reached them, followed by a couple she'd never met, the throng had cleared the stairway. "Miss Bethany, Pastor Jay, this is Elizabeth . . . sorry, I don't know your last name."

"Schmidt. And this is my husband James."

Bethany extended her hand. "We have something in common. I'm Bethany Schmidt."

"Jay Davidson." Jay shook hands with both of them. "Thanks for coming. We didn't expect an audience like this."

"James is in the siding and roofing business. They want to help with Serenity. With labor and materials."

Jay looked like he wanted to hug the guy. "Thank you. You have no idea what that means to us."

Elizabeth put her hand on Bethany's arm. "And I'd love to help with Christmas decorations. Hoover mentioned you need a tree."

Bethany felt like crying. These people were complete strangers. "That's incredibly generous. We didn't expect . . ." She stopped when she realized she was using the exact words Jay had said.

"We're just kind of giddy today and want to share the love, you know?" James looked like a five-year-old who was ready to burst if he couldn't tell his secret. "I just found out today we're having a baby. A boy. Well, probably a boy."

Elizabeth looped her arm through his. "We also almost got divorced today."

"What?" Bethany echoed Jay's question. Almost in sync, but not quite.

"Last Friday I had a doctor's appointment. I thought I had some incurable disease, but as it turned out . . ."

As she told her story—of thinking her husband didn't care or was having an affair all because of a wrong number, Bethany laughed for the first time all day. Until she glanced at Jay and saw the color literally drain from his face. "Jay? What's wrong?"

"You— your name— do they call you Beth?"

"Some people do. Why?"

"Who's your doctor?"

"Dr. Mae. Why?"

"And she was supposed to call with news on Friday afternoon at five o'clock." It was a statement, not a question, and his face continued to pale.

"Jay?"

"Th-that wrong number." He was staring at her, not James and Elizabeth.

144

"Yes?" She steadied him with a hand on his arm. "What—"

"I got it." Perspiration broke out on his upper lip.

"You got what?"

"The call. The wrong number."

Elizabeth gasped. James echoed.

"I don't under . . . stand."

"You told me to answer your phone at your place on Friday. Someone called from a Dr. M's office and said your pregnancy test was positive."

Shock froze her face until, from somewhere down by her toes, a giggle made its way up her spine, leaving a trail of goosebumps before breaking loose. "And you actually believed it was me? Jay! This whole week . . . you thought I was pregnant?"

"And you were going to give it up for adoption."

"Why would you ever think—"

"You're not. You're not pregnant." His deathly pale face suddenly flashed pink.

"Not yet." Her father put his hand on her shoulder.

"Dad." Bethany pressed her back against the railing. She took a deep breath and faced Jay. "In July, right after I moved back, I started testing to become a surrogate mother for Sarah and David. We just got the go ahead to start in vitro."

She cringed, waiting for his response. His reaction was delayed, but when it came, it was not at all what she'd expected.

Jay laughed. It started small, then grew into a contagious roar. He swooped in, picked her up, and swung her around.

"But the IVF. It could take a year, or more. We—"

He stopped, set her down, lifted her chin. "You need to know that if you were pregnant right now I'd be here for you. Because I love you. You are the kindest, most thoughtful person I have ever met. If giving your sister a baby is what you want to do, then I will hold your hand the whole way. If you want me to. Okay?"

Yes. Of course I want you to. Her mouth formed around "Okay," but nothing came out. But it didn't matter because his lips covered hers, making words unnecessary. And as he did, an angel choir broke into song.

❄

"Hey Joseph, don't freak out about asking Mary to marry you because that baby's real daddy is God and it's a boy and you have to name him Jesus because that name means he's gonna save all of us from our sins." Dante winked. "Sins like not listening good," he added in a stage whisper. The story had spread through the cast like wildfire.

Misty cleared her throat off mic, just loud enough to make Dante crack a smile. Her words floated across the overflow crowd. "All this took place to fulfill what the Lord had said through the prophet: The virgin will conceive and give birth to a son, and they will call him Immanuel. When Joseph woke up"—she paused for Jay to rise from his place on the floor—"he did what the angel of the Lord had commanded him and took Mary home as his wife."

Jay walked on steady legs, put his arm around Bethany, and led her toward the steps. On the first one, he wobbled. On purpose. She gasped. "Gotcha," he whispered into a fake and itching beard.

They walked down the aisle, between pews filled with friends and strangers—Hoover and the five men and one woman who'd postponed their Christmases to be here, James and Elizabeth, the Serenity moms, little Jerome, Hank and his new pacemaker. He glanced up at the balcony, open tonight for only two special guests—one only hours old. Jocelyn blew them a kiss. He offered a prayer of thanks as Misty read, "Back in those days, Caesar, the ruler, wanted to tax everybody, so . . ."

At the end of the aisle, Ava waited with a pillow in a black pillow case. She grinned as she held it out for Bethany to stuff under her robe. "MacKenzie told me why Jay was acting weird but he kissed you anyway so now are you guys going to get—" Bethany reached out and pinched her daughter's lips together.

Jay laughed, turned his pretend pregnant pretend wife around, and whispered, "Maybe we will, Ava. Just maybe we will."

This time when they reached the platform, a cardboard stable filled half of the stage. Beneath its roof sat the manger-style cradle handmade by an itinerant carpenter. The cradle he'd planned to give Bethany.

The organist played the first hushed notes of "You and I" and Jay reached for Bethany's hands. She smiled up at him with eyes full of trust. "You and I are only human," he sang.

"We can't do this on our own," she echoed.

"But you and I are not alone." He ran his thumb across the back of her hand. As Yolanda and the angel choir joined in, the words found a permanent place inside him. "God will guide us, help us, change us. God will change us, you and—"

Bawk! Esther hopped onto the back of the donkey, which did not wobble. But the flap of her wings turned a page in the music on the piano and the pianist fumbled and lost her place.

And Jay used the moment to squeeze Bethany's hand and whisper, "I love you"—into a live mic in dead silence.

And the angel choir giggled as Bethany answered, loud and strong. "I love you too."

❄

On Christmas morning, Elizabeth sat between James and Shannon in the fifth row of the side room at Bethlehem Community Church, dabbing her eyes with a tissue. Pastor Jay's message was titled "Don't Leave the Manger Empty." Would his words have hit her this hard if she wasn't pregnant? But if she wasn't pregnant and if the wrong person hadn't gotten the results of her pregnancy test, she wouldn't have been irritated with James and if she hadn't been frustrated at his lack of response she wouldn't have needed paint and then she wouldn't have met Shannon, and Hoover, who told her about being fearfully and wonderfully made and invited them to the Christmas program. And then she wouldn't have recognized him on TV and she and James wouldn't have decided to go to the program and offer to help rebuild Serenity. And if they hadn't done that, they wouldn't have postponed their Christmas with family to work beside these amazing people and hear the story of their crooked Christmas tree, and she wouldn't have emptied her color-coordinated bins to decorate the basement for today's dinner or donated her fiber optic trees and a box of red and white "thtockings" to Serenity and gotten a hug from little Jerome. And she wouldn't have decided to buy a doll to put in their Rudolph Red cradle every Christmas Eve.

❄

Bethany sat in the front pew, arm around Ava, trying to focus on Jay's words and not just him. She glanced at the side room where Hoover and his friends stood, ready to leave after the service. Another Christmas emergency to tend to, they'd said. Hoover wasn't sure if he'd be back. Strange man, but she missed him and Esther already.

Jay lifted the cradle that looked like a manger and set it on a table. The cradle Hoover had made for her. Because Jay had asked him to. Because Jay, rejected by his own father, had been willing to raise two children who weren't his. Could she possibly love him any more?

". . . we all have the choice. We can celebrate candy canes and colored lights and presents under the tree. Or"—Jay walked to the edge of the stage and bent down—"we can honor the Holy One who came to earth to show us who He is and how much He loves us." He lifted a tiny bundle wrapped in a shimmery white blanket. "We can celebrate the fact that"—he kissed the dark fuzz on baby Noelle's head and laid her in the manger—"for those who put their faith in Jesus Christ, the manger isn't empty. And that changes everything."

As he rocked the cradle, he smiled at Bethany. Yolanda began to sing, and a church full of people who'd made room in their inn joined in.

Said the night wind to the little lamb,
"Do you see what I see?
Way up in the sky, little lamb,
Do you see what I see?
A star, a star, dancing in the night
With a tail as big as a kite
With a tail as big as a kite."

Said the little lamb to the shepherd boy,
"Do you hear what I hear?
A song, a song, high above the trees
With a voice as big as the sea
With a voice as big as the sea."

Said the shepherd boy to the mighty king,
"Do you know what I know . . ."

Dear Reader,

Back in the day when a woman went to her doctor instead of the pharmacy to find out if she was pregnant, my husband Bill and I received some wonderful news. It was all good until the clinic sent the bill—to Bill's aunt and uncle who had a daughter who shared my name. And this Becky Melby was only fifteen years old!

Thankfully, the mix-up only resulted in a lot of laughter and a story that keeps being repeated in our family. Fast forward to this past year when I was pondering ideas for a Christmas novella. Bill, my brainstorming partner, recalled this comical event and said, "Anything you can do with that?" Oh, yeah!

When I write full-length novels, I try to be sure I don't rely on plot points that are merely misunderstandings that could be cleared up with a single conversation. For *Do You Know What I Know*, I threw out that rule and just let the story have its way. Missed signals, poor connections, wrong numbers, what ifs . . . I hope you'll agree they all work together for a cozy read.

After finishing this story, you might be left wondering who Hoover really is. Well, so am I! He and Esther wandered in uninvited and announced they were leaving again without my permission. Will they show up again next Christmas? I sure hope so. If you'd like to be notified when my next story releases, please contact me on my website: *www.beckymelby.com* or on Facebook at *https://www.facebook.com/Becky-Melby-Author-Page-147542291976020/*

I pray that in your family's Christmas celebration, the manger isn't empty and you are making room for Joy.

Blessings,
Becky

Other books by Becky Melby

Co-authored with Cathy Wienke:
Wisconsin Blessings
Minnesota Moonlight
Illinois Weddings

Novella collections:
Race to the Altar
A Door County Christmas
Cedar Creek Seasons

The Lost Sanctuary Series:
Tomorrow's Sun
Yesterday's Stardust
Today's Shadows

Wisconsin resident Becky Melby is the author of the Lost Sanctuary Series and a dozen other contemporary fiction titles. Married to her high school sweetheart for 44 years, mother of four, grandmother to fifteen, Becky thrives on writing, reading, camping, rides on the back of a silver Gold Wing, and time with family. Connect with her at www.beckymelby.com.

Discussion Questions

1. Imagine you are Mary. What would your response be when the angel appears and tells you your life is about to be turned upside down?

2. Have you experienced an "And then . . ." in your life? Could you see God's hand in it?

3. Describe a time when miscommunication threatened to damage a relationship. If you could do it over, would you handle it differently?

4. What are your thoughts on In Vitro Fertilization? Do you think Bethany was giving her sister a beautiful gift, or meddling in God's plan? (If you're discussing this in a group, be sensitive to everyone's views.)

5. Would you describe your Christmas décor as chic and sophisticated, whimsical and nostalgic, or a mixture of both? Have your tastes, like Elizabeth's, changed over the years? If so, why?

6. How would you compare Jay and Bethany's approach to dating to that of most people in their (real life) generation?

7. What was your favorite moment in *Do* You *Know What I Know?*

8. Do you sense God calling you to step out of what is known and comfortable to say yes to something you can't accomplish in your own strength?

Made in the
USA
Columbia, SC

81571355R00093